# THE ELYSIA TRILOGY

## BY

## JAY MCENERY

RATTUS NORVEGICUS ... MONKFISH ... THE BLACK DRAGON

Elysia School is the setting for the three novels of the Elysia Trilogy by Jay McEnery. Located in beautiful English countryside, with well-off, privileged students and a progressive philosophy which allows its denizens freedom to develop on their own terms, in theory it is an idyll not far removed from an earthly paradise.

In reality, however, it is a rapidly disintegrating moral wasteland, an *oubliette* of broken dreams and a breeding ground for mental disorder, sexual deviation and existential despair…

Monkfish

Part of the Elysia Trilogy

by

Jay McEnery

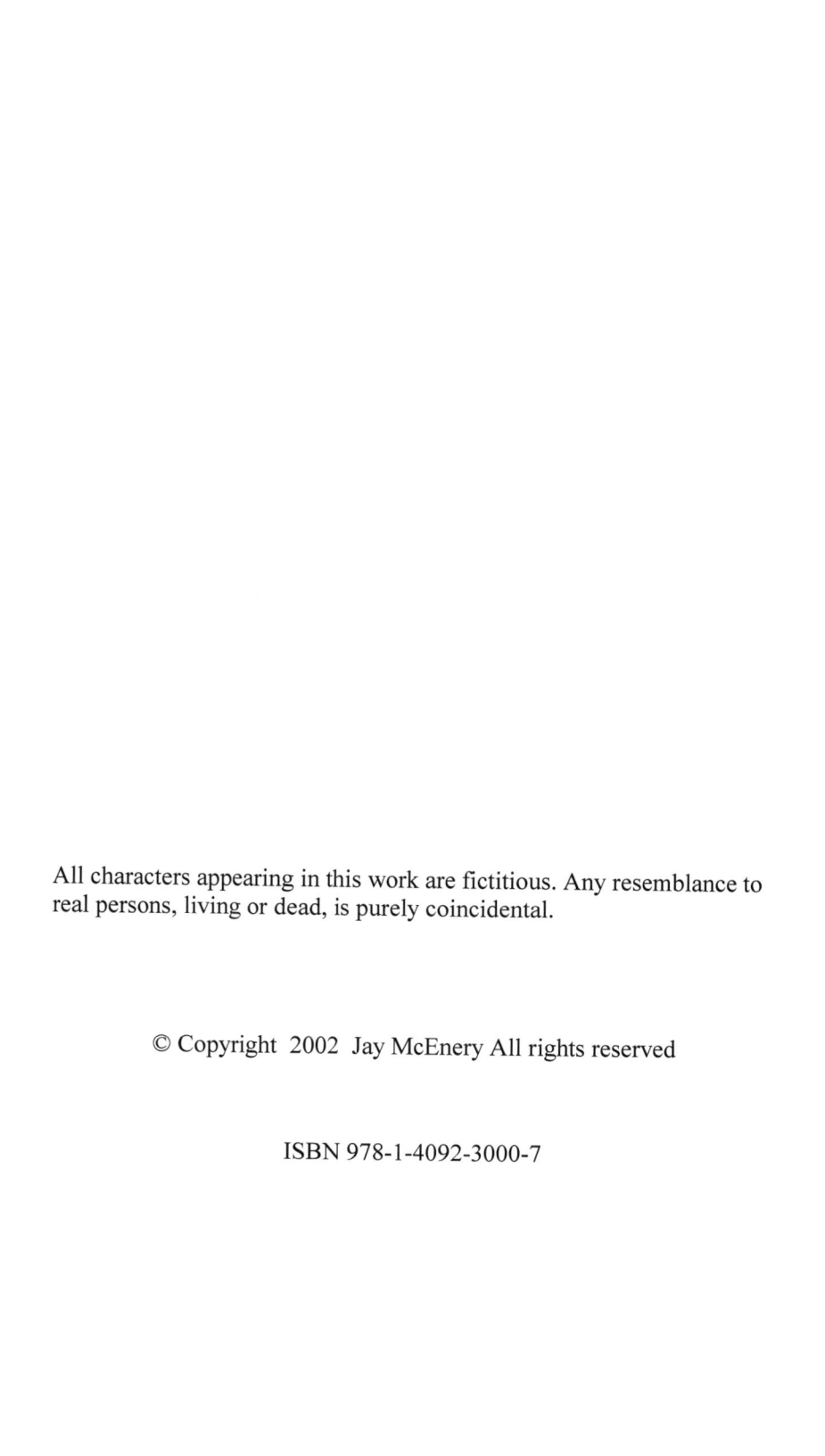

All characters appearing in this work are fictitious. Any resemblance to real persons, living or dead, is purely coincidental.

© Copyright 2002 Jay McEnery All rights reserved

ISBN 978-1-4092-3000-7

Hope is a waking dream
Aristotle

I    16 JULY 1993

ELIOT (18:35H)

Eliot was saying: "So when he hears it's needles, he practically passes out. But at the same time he can't let it go, see, he takes it to heart, thinking like anything that hurts him that much *has* to work.

So he asks where he has to put them. Well it's like everywhere; in his stomach, his earlobes, his shoulder blades. Nightmare. But this herb man is adamant: it is guaranteed to make you give up smoking. And Ed is determined to give up.

Well he doesn't trust the doctor 'cause he's an Afghan or something, so he gets him to mark the places on his body with felt-tip; then he goes out and buys the needles in some hippie shop, big needles, right, and a couple of days later, when he's got his guts together, two of us go round to help him.

First he drinks a pint of whisky, but he's still terrified and shaking; but he *insists*. It was horrible; I swear, it took us a whole night to get these things in, during which time he faints twice, is sick I don't know how many times, pisses himself, there's blood everywhere, and all the time he's just *groaning*, see. But towards dawn we get the last one in.

"Ed," I say, "it's done." So he kind of slides off the kitchen table onto the floor, tears rolling down his face and about fifty pins sticking out of him, and he goes "Oh Jesus Oh God Oh Jesus, I've done it; I did it; I MADE IT!"

And we're shaking our bloodstained heads and all, and then he gets to his feet and he's looking like a maniac, so we say, can we get you a drink or anything, and he says, "No, Eliot, I feel just fine thanks. But Eliot," he puts his shaking hand on my wrist, "for Christ's sake, give me a fag!" Jesus, we nearly died!"

In the ensuing silence, Eliot nodded several times, grinning broadly. Then he stared expectantly round the smoky room. One of his captive audience of two, his seventeen-year old cousin Jason, stared blankly up at him from the floor.

Jason had not understood a word of Eliot's story, but had been fascinated by his older cousin's shifty colourless eyes as he told it. The same eyes seemed to settle on his head now, and look pleased. With the pleasure of a hungry man who has just spotted his dinner.

Jason became quite nervous, then rapidly alarmed as he realized that his cousin had risen from his supine position on the couch and was approaching. He tried to move, but it was very difficult, and he couldn't help noticing that the light in the room had turned orange.

Suddenly, Eliot was towering over him, a fat-fingered hand reaching for his throat. Jason watched with intense distress. The hand picked up a Marlboro packet by his shoulder and extracted a cigarette.

"You don't mind?" Eliot grunted, grinning.

Jason shook his head and tried to focus on the rippling paunch around his cousin's belt. He was unable to talk. He knew that Eliot had frightened him on purpose, cunningly disguising the threat in an attempt to confuse him further. He had to get away. But how?

Eliot straightened up. "You know, I hate leaving my cigarettes in pubs," he said reflectively, and lit the cigarette with a four-inch flame from his lighter. He narrowed his eyes and looked down at Jason. "Actually, I hate it ... more than anything else."

Smoke poured through his nostrils, giving Jason an impression of demonic malice. He dared not respond.

Eliot turned to Maria, who was sitting at a straight-backed chair looking out through the French windows, one elbow on the dining table, cigarette in hand. Dressed in black, with short blonde hair and clear blue eyes, she wore a slightly puzzled look. She looked at him, met his eyes, and looked away again quickly. Her eyelids were heavy.

Eliot felt a profound sense of wellbeing. He sensed that he was in control, and power pleased him. His cousins were now where he wanted them. Especially her ... this glorious *peach* of a girl he'd last seen in a school tie and breastless three years ago. A peach. And if all went well, *his* peach. He glanced at her brother again. No, there would be no trouble from him. With a brief sigh of pleasure he reached for the sachet of white powder in his pocket. London. Night. A smart flat in Redcliffe Square and a beautiful — and stoned — chick. None of them his, but all of them his for the taking. By night, it occurred to him, everything seemed more feasible.

II   LUKE (19:41H)


Coming out of the Royal Free Hospital in Hampstead with a large white pad over one eye, Luke automatically turned downhill and walked some distance before he realized that he had no idea where he was going.

*How did I get here?*

Stopping in the middle of the pavement by the Magdala Arms, he tried to think. Some of the crowd standing outside with their beers looked at him and laughed. Noticing, Luke moved off again.

*How ... how ... remember, try!*

The doctor had terrified him. Luke's very presence had obviously offended the grey-haired man. The nurse too, had looked at him as though at something she'd just crushed under her shoe. But *why*? What had he done?

From the scratched steel bed with huge rubber wheels the first thing Luke had noticed was half a dozen birthday cards, mostly jokey ones with the punchlines invisible inside the folded card, perched on a glass cabinet. The cabinet contained syringes, kidney bowls, and ominous steel instruments.

*He couldn't have been all bad if people sent him cards.*

The doctor had pounced with fearfully strong fingers to the wound on his head.

"Please ... " Luke had whispered, terrified of pain. But his throat had convulsed and made him unable.

"What happened?"

"Fall ... fell ... "

"Drunk."

"N ... "

"It's on your breath. Keep still."

Such hatred!

He had nearly passed out when the two shadowy faces bent over him. Perhaps he had passed out. Then there had been excruciating pain, but in some ways a relief when it actually started. Then, suddenly, he had found himself propped up on both feet, tottering, blind in one eye. He had noticed the tufts of grey hair in the doctor's ears.

Under the contemptuous eyes of what seemed to be a large proportion of the hospital staff he had left without another word.

Now he wasn't even sure where he was going. His flat was in Redcliffe Square, he recalled, miles away, and furthermore there was something he had to remember — which he couldn't — before he went back there. The image of Eliot crossed his mind, but he made no connections.

But if he was in Hampstead, his father's house was quite close. His father, he remembered, had recently gone abroad, but the maid would probably be in. She could lend him money. He would go there.

Dorothy, fortunately, was able to recognize him, though not his slurred voice, on the video entry-phone. She activated the gates and met him at the door. Her first words were: "Oh my Lord, Lukey, what on earth have you done to yourself?" in her oddly distressing Scottish burr.

"Want bath." Luke muttered. "Want drink."

After he had swallowed a brandy in the drawing room, he felt the edge of his dread recede. Dorothy watched him with pallid alarm. "Dad here?" he asked, replenishing his glass.

"He went to America on Tuesday. But you *know* that."

"Uh huh."

"Oh, Lukey: someone called for you earlier."

Luke did a double take. "Who?"

"Someone called Eliot."

Luke frowned. "What did he want?"

"He said to remind you that he'd be at Ding ... Ding ... "

"Ding?"

"Dong ... "

"Dong?" Luke tried to sound impatient as his father would have done.

"Ding ... dong." Luke's eyes widened. She was making fun of him.

"Dingles, or was it Dongles, he said to remind you that he'd be there tonight."

"Dingwall's!" Luke breathed easier.

"Dingle's. Tonight."

"OK." He eyed Dorothy with renewed wonder, querying for the upteenth time why his father had employed this woman. The only thing you could say about her was that she could be insulted with impunity. Even he could manage it. Well, perhaps that was it ... in fact, of course it was! What a delicious purchase, a human being whom one could insult without fear. Luke had a sudden flash of respect for his father and swallowed a third brandy in his honour.

"Right. I'm going to have a bath now, then I'm going out." He explained. "Find me a clean shirt and stuff ... " He hesitated. Dorothy stared at him. " ... Please."

Dorothy nodded and went off.

Luke was beginning to feel better as he strode from the drawing room, up the stairs, where the walls were lined with posters of films his father had financed. He was beginning to wish he'd said something to the doctor, something along the lines of "Listen you sham of cock I'm paying for the fucking national health service and I expect some respect." After he had finished with his head, of course.

He went into the marble-tiled bathroom and began to run water from the gold taps. There was a full length mirror wrapped around the sunken bath area, and he stared at himself in it now. Five foot six, emaciated and white. But with a good head of long, curly black hair and a face that would have been chubby if he hadn't forgotten to eat for most of the last six months — since, in fact, his father had come to the conclusion that it was time he made his own way in the world and bought him the flat in Redcliffe Square.

Not a bad face. With a massive hunk of cotton wool obscuring the upper left quadrant. Someone had once said that he looked like Rasputin on acid on a bad trip. He hadn't known who Rasputin was.

Strangely calmed by the huge hypnotic eyes staring back at him he forced himself to concentrate, to think back.

*You must remember! You MUST!*

With a supreme effort he steadied his thoughts. He had arrived at the hospital in a taxi. A taxi from a restaurant ... like some impenetrable fog slowly rising, the memory returned; first, the hamburger and champagne at the underground restaurant in Covent Garden; then, the sickening discovery of the single pink twenty in his pocket, not the ten or more he expected to have.

The horror.

Followed by the realization that he was very near the door in a packed and busy restaurant.

And finally, the obscure and improbable decision to do a runner.

And the event itself. The nonchalant stroll towards the door. The "Excuse me, sir," behind him. A rush of adrenalin, the crucial moment of decision, and the leap. Surprise at how reluctantly his limbs and respiratory system responded to the emergency; noise behind; the flight through the open door and onto the pavement, then — his big mistake — a glance back; and like a bolt from the sky the crunch of the lamppost knocking him senseless. He could recall grimly hanging on as he slid down it, then suddenly being jerked upwards inches before touching the ground, and being turned ... and a voice gasping, "Oh, Shit ... " And then someone had lifted him, pushed him, another disembodied voice said "God Almighty, what've you done to him?" A hand in his groin and the vague comprehension that someone was feeling in his pocket and extracting the lone twenty. And then he was in a taxi, and now he was here. Penniless. And why had it happened?

*Because despite his most consummate fear, some ghastly corner of him was driven to seek it out.*

And

*Because it simply hadn't occurred to him to send out for more money.*

He remembered all this whilst staring into his own eyes.

*But he had remembered, Thank God!*

They had laughed at him, that time when Rasputin had been mentioned. And they had laughed even louder when he'd asked the identity of this unknown twin.

"Don't mess with me." He ordered menacingly to the mirror, straightening himself to his full height and pointing a threatening finger. "Just DON'T fucking mess with me."

III  MARTIN (20:05H)


Martin parked his car in Maxwell Road. It was a fine, warm evening. He retrieved a small polythene bag from under the driving seat and took an unhurried walk down Fulham Broadway.

There was a good deal of traffic. It was on account of this, and the concentration needed to dodge some of the more light-headed pedestrians, that he nearly missed the white Sierra parked about three doors down from where he was going. The bored looking man in the black Belstaff jacket was smoking and tapping with the fingers of his free hand on the sill of his open window. Martin looked, more out of habit than suspicion, and then he saw it: the little cream earplug, it's wire light against the man's neck.

He did not alter his pace, or his expression. Nor did he look at the man directly again, after the first glance. He walked straight past the house he wanted, and continued to the end of the road.

The fear, as before, pounced so swiftly he didn't see it coming. And although it was not the first time, he was stunned by the force of it. It wasn't just the sensation of fear, it was its complete victory. It made him feel like some small shamed child, as though he had suddenly lost all control. His overwhelming desire was to run to a doorway, curl up and let them come and get him. And the strange thing, he managed to reflect, was that through his fear he had the strength or whatever it was to laugh at himself, or rather at this creature that was not himself.

Without looking back, he turned left into Barclay Street, a residential road with a terraced row of Georgian houses.

It eased slightly as he turned the corner. He was again able to think. It was the third time this year.

He forced himself to concentrate on the matter in hand, and counted eight houses down. All his instincts told him to run. He fought them down. But the fight, he noticed through the nightmare, came no easier with experience. He mounted the stairs to the eighth house and examined its doorbell. It wasn't right, so he went on to the ninth. This looked better.

There were four bells on the entryphone system, each with a name inscribed. Martin glanced up to see which lights were on then rang the top one, a Mr Colin Trotman, and waited. There was no answer. He then pressed the bottom bell, took a deep breath, and after a few seconds there was a crackle from the machine and a male voice.

"Yes?" it asked.

"Colin!" Martin said.

"No, I think you've got the wrong flat. You want number four," the crackly voice replied shortly.

"Oh, I'm sorry," Martin said, emulating an American accent, then waited five seconds after the intercom went dead and rang the bell again. "Oh, shit, I'm so sorry," he said when the man answered again, audibly irritated. After another ten seconds he rang again.

"Hello? Look, I hate to trouble you again, I don't know if I'm ringing the wrong bell or if it's broken or something, but Colin's not answering and I can see his lights are on, would you mind ... ?"

There was no answer this time, just the buzz of the mortice being drawn electronically. Martin pushed the door open and stepped in.

At the end of a long corridor, the stairs ran, as he had hoped, up the back of the building. He made for them and started climbing. Three flights up, he stopped by a window that gave on to the gardens behind the house, then another garden, then the backs of the houses on Fulham Broadway.

Almost directly opposite was the window he was looking for.

Besides Barney, there were two unfamiliar men in the kitchen area. Both wore white shirts and their hair, unlike Barney's, was short. One leant against the kitchen sink, one sat at Barney's blue formica table. It was impossible to see whether they were talking or just sitting there.

Martin descended the stairs after a minute and met a middle-aged man clasping an open Evening Standard at the bottom. Martin smiled brightly and the man frowned.

"Sorry to have bothered you. He's not in — I guess that's why he never answered his bell; thanks again." The man examined Martin's smart suit and watched him leave in silence.

Outside, Martin continued down Barclay Street. Then he turned into Effier Street and reaching the Fulham Road returned to his car.

\* \* \*

He drove up the North End Road, then turned west towards Hammersmith. After a while he stopped by a phone box. From here he called the house he had just looked at. The phone rang three times.

"Barney?"

"Martin?" Barney spoke briskly, but sounded calm.

"Barney, is that you?"

"Yeah." A pause. "What's up, Mart?" Martin hesitated, controlling his voice.

"Barney, I've run into some problems. I'm going to be a little late coming by."

"OK. No problem."

"I don't want to mess up your plans. If you're going out, or having people round, we can…"

"No, no no, nothing"

"You're sure?"

"Nothing. Home alone. Just get over when you can, Mart. I'll wait up for you."

"Right ... I'll see you then."

He waited for, and heard, two clicks before replacing his receiver. He now felt a new flash of cold at the back of his neck. It was a mild burst of the fear, but this time, he didn't worry too much about it. He knew it was justified.

He dialled again.

"Scotland Yard." A voice answered. Martin quoted an extension number and waited. A woman's voice answered.

"Superintendent Walters, please. Martin calling, please tell him it's urgent."

"Is that ... Martin, or *Mr* Martin?"

"Just tell him Martin. He'll know who I am." The line went silent. Martin let the tension flow, not fighting it.

"Hello?" The voice came back.

"Yes, hello?"

The voice was prim. "Superintendent Walters says he doesn't know you, actually, and unfortunately he can't speak to you now. Can I take a message?" There was a pause. "Hello?"

"Hello; I'm sorry: did you ask him personally?"

"Yes." The voice turned irritable. "Look, do you want to leave a message or not?"

But no answer was forthcoming. Martin had replaced the receiver. His hand was shaking.

## IV  MARIA (22:00H)

Eliot led the way out of the flat in Redcliffe Square, Jason's last cigarette hanging from his mouth, leather jacket slung carelessly over his shoulder.

Jason followed him out onto the street with less confidence. Maria came last.

Jason felt as though he was about to be sick. The very last thing he wanted was to leave the flat, but he no longer had the confidence to say so. He knew that taking drugs was a mistake. He was beginning to think coming to London in the first place was a mistake. But there was of course *a reason*. He now held on to this reason with both hands.

"Slam the door ... " Eliot called back over his shoulder. Jason hung back to perform this task, then hurried after his sister, already alongside Eliot.

She turned briefly and watched him stumble over, noting the greenish pallor in his cheeks. She knew he was in a bad way. She knew she should help him — or at least say something. Most of her wanted to do just that. Normally, she wouldn't have hesitated. She was always more like an older sister than a younger. But this time, she didn't. She felt a confusing mixture of shame and irritation.

Eliot, on the other hand, was very much enjoying himself. When his aunt had rung a week ago to say that Jason had just finished his A-Levels and was looking for a holiday job in television and could he help, he had been deeply annoyed. At first he had tried fobbing her off with the line that the television industry was as tight as it had ever been, and even a person in his position, etc. etc.. The aunt, never one to give up easily, had announced that whatever, Jason and his sister (who had just taken her GCSEs) would be travelling up to London at the weekend, and wouldn't it be nice if they could all meet anyway as they hadn't seen each other for such a long time. Eliot had said that he'd probably be away, but that he'd let them know.

As the weekend drew closer Eliot, whose real occupation was more or less nothing and just then absolutely nothing, realized that meeting his cousins was a potential diversion. He was also aware that Aunt Harriet and her husband were increasingly wealthy on account of a thriving caravan park in Broadstairs, and doted on their children. By the by, it had occurred to him that there was at least one good evening's entertainment to be got out of them if he played his cards right.

So far, it had all gone according to plan. Luke had lent him money and acquiesced in the use of his flat (he seemed to acquiesce in most things now, Eliot noted, wondering if the missing drugs would be remarked on), and since meeting Jason and Maria at Victoria that afternoon, Jason had paid for some excellent sinsemilla and supper at the Assoifé in Kensington Park Road. If his luck just held, he was thinking, if ...

He led them now towards Redcliffe Gardens in search of a taxi, his ego flying high. He was too rarely able to indulge himself these days and doing so, combined with the stimulating effects of the fifty-ones, had put him in a fine mood.

A cab was hailed, and Eliot allowed Maria to climb in first.

"Dingwalls." He told the driver. Then he turned to his other cousin and had to restrain a malevolent grin.

"All right, Jason?" Jason had been expecting someone to talk to him and willing them not to. But he held on grimly to the central motivator in his brain: his mother had told him, innocently (having got it from Eliot's own mother, who was equally innocent), that Eliot was in TV and could introduce him to the right people. If you wanted something, as his father said, you had to work for it ...

"Dumb fuck." Eliot thought, nodding cheerfully back at his inanely grinning cousin. "Loser." He added forgetting for a second his own status. He was seated on the flip seat, opposite Maria, and when the cab rolled round a corner, he found his knee pressed against hers. She looked out of the window most of the time, smiling slightly — a fact which Eliot found prepossessingly attractive.

In fact, if Eliot could have read her mind, he would have been delighted beyond all expectation. She had felt his heavy leg against her thigh, and felt something that amazed her: she liked it. As she stared out the window, she compared two thoughts. First was the question, if she wanted to feel attracted to Eliot, her banal and arrogant cousin, why shouldn't she? The second was complete disbelief and incomprehension of the first. She wondered if it could be the drugs which, again to her surprise, she had willingly accepted. But she thought not. Her mind was so clear, her feelings so precise and somehow *natural*, logical, that she was sure it was more *her* than the drugs. But in that case — what on earth had happened to her?

The cab stopped at Camden Lock. Jason paid the fare automatically. Eliot had explained earlier — straight away in fact — that a sudden emergency had emptied his current account and so he was going to be broke until Monday, a story Jason assumed to be a lie though he had by no means gauged the extent of the deception. Money meant little — it was his mother's anyway and he was far more concerned with the state of his head.

He now patiently paid thirty pounds in entrance fees, was ushered past the bouncers at the low front door to the club and was immediately directed to the bar by Eliot.

The band had not yet come on; but loud recorded music was pounding through the long, low room. There was a fair crowd, but no one Eliot recognized. In any case virtually everyone except Luke now deliberately avoided him. This fact had a lot to do with money.

"Do you come here much?" Maria shouted above the din.

"Oh, you know," Eliot tried to look blasé, "it depends what's on. It's a pretty good place for music as they go." In fact they'd come because Luke had intimated that he might drop by later and Eliot had mentioned the "old school friend whose dad's in the movies" to Jason.

"I like it." Maria said. She was swaying slightly to the sound of the music and looking with interest around her.

A peach. "Yeah, yeah, it's not bad." Eliot submitted, leaning against a red pillar. He was pleased, with himself and with his younger cousin. Already he had noticed glances from the crowd and some of the attention brushed off on him. It was going to be a good evening, he decided. Especially if he could just get his lips round that unbearably fresh peach. "Oh God," he prayed again, "it's my turn. It must be. *Please*!"

## V   SUZANNE (22:15H)

"Father's just bought last year's Derby winner."

"Bought him? What on earth do you mean?"

"I mean he's paying for his sperm. He's having Aladdin's Lady bonked by him."

"How extraordinary. How much does that cost?"

"Oh, I don't know. Fifty to a hundred thou I should imagine."

Suzanne listened with one ear to the conversation on her left. The conversation on her right also had something to do with horses and she half-listened to that too.

Entering the house in Ebury Street, she'd taken one look at the Stubbses and the riding boots in the hall — a whole row of about six pairs, all gleaming, and realized that she'd probably made a mistake. Then she'd heard the baying laughter and been met by a grinning Rupert wearing a tuxedo and a high wing collar. His accent had refined itself a couple of notches since she'd first heard it at a party two weeks ago. "Darling!" he said. "So glad you could make it. Come on in and meet the crowd." His breath already smelt strongly of alcohol. Looking away, she noticed a full size painting of a pompous-looking man that took up much of the corridor. He wore a red coat and a bowler hat.

"Your father?"

"That's the old man." Rupert agreed. "Gone up to Gloucester for the weekend. We've got the place to ourselves." He attempted a wink at this point, but it came out more like a leer. Suzanne ignored it.

In the sitting room she found three other female guests. Although young they were heavily made up, big fans of the fishnet and choker school. They were all smoking. There were a liberal number of Bollinger and Johnnie Walker bottles scattered around — and of course, the inevitable white powder. Behind the strident laughter and cheerless grinning, all of them looked up at her somewhat furtively as she entered.

Rupert also had four male guests, and it became clear that they had all been to school together. Three, like Rupert, were thick-set, rugby players. The fourth was thinner and seemed less at ease, as though fearing the others might decide to pick on him at any moment. An ingenue, Suzanne decided, like herself. She lit a cigarette and sat down to wait for the awful irritation of having to listen to people you disliked.

She'd been with someone from the City when she'd met Rupert. "A quiet affair," he'd said. "Just a few friends if you happen to be free." And she had accepted. Despite everything she still had hope. Well, this was the last time.

Dinner was a desultory affair. Rupert and his friends had pooled their culinary skills and come up with a predictable chilli con carne. The conversation meandered from the topic of horses to that of house prices in the Home Counties, and then back again. No one seemed interested in the food.

"Right then," Rupert spoke sharply. "How about a game?" The suggestion sent a tremor of expectation round the room. Suzanne realized with a sudden, slightly shocked amusement, what it was all about. Why she was here. She looked at Rupert. Sure enough, he was grinning down his long red nose at her, the meaning apparent in his dilated eyes.

A few excited voices commended the idea. "Bunnies and hares!" one of the girls said eagerly.

"Bunnies and hares?" Rupert repeated. People began to stand up.

"Who hides first then, bunnies or hares?"

"Bunnies!"

"Hares!"

"Bunnies it is."

"Where are the scarves?" a girl asked. "Scarves in the trunk in my bedroom. Andrew, you get them." As people began to get up, Rupert leant over Suzanne. He had consumed a great quantity of alcohol and was bleary-eyed. It was possible, for a moment, to see how he would look when he was fifty.

"Do you know this game, Suzanne?" he asked when they were alone.

"I think I can guess. And I'm afraid it's not really for me. I'm sorry."

"Don't you want to hear the rules?"

"No, thanks."

Rupert licked his lips. "The bunnies, that's you and the other girls, go off first and hide, and when you've hidden you have to put a blind-fold on so that you can't see. Then, the hares, which is me and the other fellows, come and look for you. When you're found you'll be touched by whoever finds you, and you have to guess who it is. With the blindfold on."

He stared hard at her and Suzanne nodded. "And every time you make a bad guess, the catcher can either take a piece of your clothing off, or kiss you. You get the idea." It was clear that he was growing excited even at the rules. Then you swap roles." Rupert sat back and stared at her. The harsh laughter of the others was audible in the distance.

"What fun," she said softly.

"It can be a lot of fun. A lot of fun."

"Unfortunately, I ... "

"You're a sporting lady, Suzanne. I could tell when I saw you. I should know. I'm an expert." He grinned with perfect self-confidence.

"No. You're wrong."

"Really? You came here didn't you?"

"I came to dinner. That's what you invited me for."

Rupert's mouth congealed into a mocking grin. "Wouldn't mind fucking you," he said casually. "Stay, and you'll have a good time. But perhaps you're scared ... you wouldn't be the first." He shrugged.

Suzanne stared at him expressionlessly.

"If you're scared, you'd better go now."

"Thank you. I will." She began to get up.

Rupert's hand reached out and grabbed her by the wrist. She was aware of a considerable strength behind the hand, and he grinned, knowing it. "I said I'd like to fuck you, Suzanne."

"Goodbye."

The grip did not weaken. "Maybe my desire'll get too strong for me. Maybe I'll have to *make* you stay."

"Don't imagine," Suzanne said, "that you're scaring me. Let go of my arm."

Rupert let her go, still leering and breathing heavily.

"I'll show myself out," she said, quite calmly, knowing what they didn't know.

As she passed through the double doors into the candle-lit hall, two of the male guests looked at her.

"Going?" one of them asked. Suzanne nodded without stopping. But before she could reach the door, a third man appeared and blocked her way. "Excuse me," he said. "I was meaning to ask; are you foreign?" Suzanne heard chortling behind her. "I only ask because you seem — you know — quite darkish."

"My father is Colombian." Suzanne replied, looking him in the eye. She noticed that one of the girls had reappeared behind the man, and was staring at her now with an odd, unpleasant glare.

"Colombian? Oh, what, is he a drug dealer then?"

Suzanne felt her throat tighten. "What did you say?" The man in front of her smirked. "Isn't that what you Colombians are all about?"

"My father is a United Nations diplomat." She took a step forward. The man in front of her did not move. Behind her she heard Rupert say, "Strange, I thought these Colombians were all so full of happy dust they'd do anything!" His friends guffawed. Suzanne turned and saw the hungry arrogance in their eyes. Her sudden fury almost made her faint. These people had somehow focused all her burning anger; all the pain and sheer bitter yearning for vengeance seemed to be forcing itself out of every pore. She surveyed the four gargoyle-like faces around her. "It's not worth it." She thought, desperately trying to contain herself. "Get out."

But for the first time the thought did not prevail. And the result was elation. The first she could remember in months.

"All right," she said, "I'll play your game." One of the men cheered.

She wandered upstairs with the scarf she had been given loose in one hand. The other girls scrambled back and forth around her, giggling and shrieking in excitement and anticipation. Whenever one of them caught her eye, she saw mild intrigue mixed with contempt. And also dislike, because even now, she was still beautiful. She paid them no attention and found a child's bedroom with a small bed and a Wendy house to "hide" in. Then there was a cry of "tally-ho!" from below, a muffled shriek from a nearby room, and the heavy thud of boots on stairs.

It took about five minutes for Rupert to find her. He pulled up the flap of the Wendy house and stared. "You're cheating," he exclaimed, seeing the blindfold in her hand. "There's a penalty for that."

"Just get on with it."

He came towards her with a grin. Suzanne watched thinking even then that there was still time to turn back.

First his hands went for her breasts. A flush coloured his cheeks as he pulled the flesh free of her sweater. The lump in his pants expanded. Then his fingers were struggling with the clasp of her belt. She waited, wondering at the bestiality of these people. That certain type of public school, irrevocably led to this. Bestiality. Weird.

One strong yank took her skirt and underwear down around her knees. He yanked further and they slipped over her ankles. Seeing her nakedness she felt a quick flute of nausea. But there was no turning back now. He was groping forward, hands coming down behind her shoulders. A brief pause to remove his own clothes, and the thick wedge of his cock was revealed, shivering.

And then he was down, shoving against her with short, sharp grunts.

She parted her legs and then he was in her. He held her tight as he grunted, moving only his midriff. She thought about what she was doing, and couldn't fathom it. How had her nature come to this? He had turned sweaty, and she could feel herself getting damp. His hands returned to her breasts for a second, at least allowing her to breathe. He was moving faster, harder against her. Revenge, what a strange thing. She, who would have been the last ... now the first ...

It took less time than she expected. The sweep of wetness and the sudden grind of bone against bone was the end of it. And then he was gasping for air. And then he was out, staring at her suspiciously. The animal after the bowl of water. Not grateful. Just suspicious — as well he might be. "Bitch." He murmured. Then he rose, recovered his underwear and left the room without a backward glance. Suzanne pulled her skirt back towards her and wondered whether it was enough. But she found herself ready for more.

All four of them found her. Only one, the shy one, murmured: "Do you mind if we don't?"

She left the house with a note tucked under the door: "Welcome to HIV".

## VI  CHLOE, ETC. (23:40H)

Eliot was dancing up by the stage with Maria when Chloe entered Dingwalls. With her was her date, a writer whom she had met at a publisher's party a week before, and her date's friend, a gay Scot, with whom he had mysteriously appeared at the Szechuan restaurant earlier that evening. The friend, she observed with incredulity, had just put on a pair of sunglasses.

The band was coming on. Big, ugly, scantily clad black men in costumes that looked to be circa '71. The guitarist, swinging his Strat from the hip, was bald and had a giant silver earring in his right ear. Only the harmonica player, who was older and wore a white suit and a panama over his salt and pepper hair looked like he had anything to do with the blues. His face was lined and wry, his eyes hickory stained and bloodshot. He gazed into the audience with a largely untoothed grin.

"All right then, people. Let's see if we can't get y'all laid tonight, all right? I said Awwwwwwwwwwwwwright!"

Chloe was separated from the band by a raised podium where more people stood and watched. She could see them on video screens above the bar and these she glanced at without special interest. To her right the club was emptying as people made their way toward the band. "Shall we get a table?" one of her companions called above the noise. She ignored him. She was irritated with both of them — one for bringing a friend, the other for being that friend.

* * *

Jason was standing by the bar; in fact he had more or less monopolized a corner of it and was drinking fast, more through nervousness than any desire to get drunk. People kept looking at him in odd ways, and he was thinking that what he felt was basically fear, though he couldn't say why. All he knew was that he was out of his depth, he didn't belong here, and if he ever got out intact he'd never leave Broadstairs or touch drugs again. The thought filled him with nauseous self-loathing; he wanted nothing more than to leave now; but he hadn't the courage to go on his own.

* * *

Feelings like this were well-known to Luke. But as he shuffled unsteadily from the ticket office, past the bouncers and into the shuddering building, he was feeling something else too: mind-numbing fatigue. The journey down had been rough; he'd knocked the bandage off his head in the taxi, and it wouldn't stick on again. At that point he'd also realized that the clothes Dorothy had fetched for him weren't just baggy, they were his father's, who happened to be three inches taller than him. His head was swimming, revolving, even, judging from the view from his remaining eye, and he knew that there was only one relief; more drugs. On account of the state he was in, he was inclined to think that his eyes or mind might be failing when the first person he saw was Chloe. She was talking sneeringly to a man at the bar. And Luke suddenly heard, quite clearly, the word Charles. "Charles," she was saying. "I will not drink that crap. Get me a *real* beer." It was the final, surreal straw. He moaned vaguely, and felt his knees buckle. When he opened his eyes, he found himself leaning against a cold red pillar, a sledgehammer thumping him on the back; Chloe was directly in front of him, staring.

"All right now, mate?" a disembodied voice said behind him. Luke nodded, and the thumping stopped. Chloe shook her head.

Luke blinked and said out of a dream: "What are you doing here?"

Chloe pursed her lips. "Luke. Luke ... Badminton."

"Ballingham."

"So you're still alive."

"Haven't seen *you* for a while!" Luke replied anxiously. He wasn't sure what she had said, not hearing her through the violent rendition of "Louie Louie" shaking the room. Her look of incredulity was making him nervous. Her eyes seemed to be drilling through his skull ...

In fact she was wondering why he had a tie and a pad of cotton wool tied around his head. "What's that on your head?" She demanded.

"Yes," Luke agreed deafly, shaking his head. "I thought I was too." Even as he spoke, somewhere deep in the mists of his mind a thought tried to surface, a thought that concerned Chloe and might be important. But it gave up long before it reached consciousness and returned to obscurity.

Chloe suddenly laughed and took some cigarettes out of her jeans. "You're out of your mind, aren't you Luke?"

"As a matter of fact, yes ... oh, could I have one?"

She offered the packet of Marlboro. "Here alone?"

"I'm looking for Eliot. Have you seen him?"

"Eliot? *Jesus*, is he here — or d'you know two people with that stupid name?"

"I hope so. Thanks. How about you?"

"I've got company. One's gone to see the band. The other's trying to get served. Useless."

"Listen. I've got to find Eliot, otherwise I'm going to pass out. I'll come back." Luke waved a rapid goodbye. Chloe watched him go. She

29

had felt a small trickle of interest at the sight of him. But mostly just irritation. Most things made her irritated now, one way or another.

\* \* \*

The crowd pushed forward on Maria and Eliot, Eliot pressed against Maria's back. They were only a couple of yards from the knee high stage, and she seemed to lean into him. He'd had a couple of beers on Jason and was beginning to feel invincible. As though to balance himself in the melee, he put his hands on her waist. Her bottom swayed against his pelvis and he felt a wild stirring of lust. The guitarist counted into the next riff, the lights flashed and the crowd surged.

Maria felt the stirring too, and her heart beat faster. Then, quite suddenly Eliot's touch was disengaged. She turned and saw her cousin pumping the hand of a white-faced youth, expensively though absurdly dressed in clothes much too big for him. He was visibly sagging at the knees, wore a bizarre, piratical contraption round his head and was muttering something which Eliot was clearly trying to catch. Then Eliot turned back to her and shouted in one ear: "Pop out. See you in a minute."

Maria was feeling strange. The drugs she'd been given, added to the excitement of new sights and sounds had done something to her. She wasn't sure about the propriety of her cousin's behaviour but two things were uppermost in her mind: first, it didn't seem to matter, and second, she was enjoying it. She was dimly aware that she ought to draw the line; equally dimly she sensed that something in her was fighting the "ought to". The warmth of the body at her back had been so pleasant, the tingling sensation in her teeth so nice, the line was getting ever further away.

\* \* \*

Eliot was selfish and greedy. But he was also shrewd, and therefore well aware that the best thing going for him was Luke's existence and general sponsorship. He was also intelligent enough to know that Luke's estimation of him would drop further if he denied having drugs on him rather than just handing them over, regardless of the fact that they were Luke's anyway and basically stolen. He therefore guided Luke to the toilets, bundled the two of them into a cubicle (to no one's particular interest) and took out his little silver box. Without further ado, Luke freebased a pinch on the edge of the blade then snorted a pair of thick lines which Eliot cut for him. Luke's gratitude was palpable.

"Oh, man ... " he breathed. "Didn't think I was going to make it."

Eliot grunted and had a quick line himself, while Luke noisily cleared his nose.

"Who's the girl?" Luke demanded when he was finished.

"Maria." Eliot stuck his thumb in his nose and sniffed. "Cousin."

"Cousin?" Luke considered. "Is that ... legal?"

Eliot got up as Luke slid to a sitting position on the bowl. "Who cares? Anyway, what the fuck happened to your head?"

"Oh ... " Luke sighed, remembering. "Runner, no money. Eliot, did I give you some money earlier?"

Eliot calculated. "Yes, you did. Why, is there a problem?"

"No. Not any more. I just needed to know."

"I'll pay you back, you know that."

Eliot grew restless.

"Hey, listen, Luke. I want you to meet my other cousin, Jason. The one I told you about the other day. The TV one, OK?"

Luke frowned darkly. "You told me about him?"

"Right. He's somewhere near the bar. You all right now?" Luke nodded, stood up and reached for the latch. Then he fell over again.

"Babar did it, anyway," he mumbled thoughtfully, as Eliot helped him up. Eliot assumed he was rambling and patted him on the shoulder.

As they rejoined the melee outside, Luke remembered.

"Guess who I just bumped into?"

"Who?"

"Chloe."

"What, Chloe, fuck it if it moves, drink it if it doesn't?"

"Yeah."

"Chloe; well, well. Must be five years. Still the same great tits?"

VII

Martin tried not to listen to the conversation on his left: "No, it was a firework. Blew his arm off and he bled to death. Uruguay. What? Of course it wasn't Guy Fawkes night, Uruguay I said! Well I don't know what Paul was doing in Uruguay, I thought you might!" There was a pause, then a burst of group laughter.

A riverboat ploughed down the Thames below. Nadeine came up next to him and watched it. He turned to her. In the six months they had known each other, he had never seen her eyes angry or sad, anything in fact besides the strange misty mixture of cool and warm.

"By the way," she said, "can I take a couple more grams off you ... on credit?"

Martin nodded.

"Thanks. Can you manage a dozen?"

"Yes."

"I'll be cutting down soon, don't worry."

Martin had heard it before and normally let it pass. Today he didn't. He said neutrally: "I know you sell it to your friends. If you want money, you can ask for that too."

Nadeine gave him a quizzical glance with something indefinable

33

mixed in with it. Then she laughed. "I don't *ask* people for money," she said. "Ever."

Martin met her stare. And suddenly a very strange idea occurred to him.

A tall, blonde young man with several gold rings detached himself from a group and strolled towards them. Now he made as if to kiss Nadeine. She allowed him to peck her cheek. Martin was cold with his new thought. "Karl." Nadeine said. "This is Martin."

"Enchanted." Karl said in a high-pitched voice. Martin nodded.

"Your party is wonderful, my dear," Karl said. "Dinner was delicious." Nadeine took the cigarette from his fingers and smoked it. "You should cut that out," Karl said, pleased. "It'll turn your lungs black."

Nadeine shrugged. No one's going to see them."

Karl laughed heartily. After a moment he turned to Martin. "Haven't I seen you at Oxford?"

"It's possible."

"Christchurch?"

"I wasn't at college."

"Ahhh ... I remember. The Travelling Salesman!" Karl chuckled and looked at Nadeine for support. She raised an eyebrow and looked at Martin. He took a sip from his drink. Apparently encouraged, Karl said: "I think I had some of your stuff once. Not bad. Fascinating career. He glanced sidewize at Martin. "But ... "

"I'm sorry." Martin said to Nadeine. "Tonight, I can't be bothered with this prick." Karl turned crimson and opened his mouth, but Nadeine stopped him. She put a hand on his arm and murmured something. His face glowing, Karl turned away.

"You *are* in a bad mood." Nadeine said. "And now poor Karl is unhappy. He was so cheerful earlier. A summer spread in Vogue. Poor Karl."

"Something tells me he'll survive."

Nadeine ignored him, still watching Karl. He had draped himself over the deck balustrade and was looking miserably down at the Thames.

"He's clever ... a self-made man. But he hates to be put down, because he knows he can be put down. Real status means being born lucky." She turned to Martin and smiled, not entirely sweetly. "And that, you know, Martin, means being born rich."

VIII

"Cos I ain't had no loving ...
seeeence my Baby been gone ..."

And the harmonica wailed a lament. As Luke and Eliot squeezed through the crowd, first back to Maria, and then all together across the podium, they met Chloe. She and her two friends had found a table. Seeing each other she and Eliot nodded, neither very enthusiastically.

"Why don't you join us?" the Scot said cheerfully, seeing that they knew each other. "Pull up some chairs." Everyone hesitated. Then Eliot said: "Sure. I've just got to find my cousin Jason. Maria, why don't you stay here with Luke?"

Luke shrugged and pulled a chair over. Maria did the same. Luke introduced them as far as he was able. Chloe then introduced her own friends, both of whom tried not to look too curiously at Luke. Before long, everyone was watching the band again. Chloe, however, was interested in Maria.

"You're with Eliot," she said bluntly.

"Yes." Maria agreed.

Chloe made a face which left no one in doubt of her opinion of that. Maria stared at her curiously. "How do you all know each other?" She wondered.

"We all got to spend several years in the same hothouse."

"Oh ... Elysia?"

"I suppose Eliot's told you what a hit he was there?"

"Sort of. But it closed down, he said."

"Some car company bought it, turned it into a management training school." At that moment Eliot returned to the table with Jason. Between them, they carried a dozen or so cans of Schlitz. Chloe rolled her eyes. "So, Chloe," he muttered through the pumping music. "Long time no see. How you been?" Chloe shrugged.

"Here we are," said Eliot. "Let me introduce you all." Jason stared with dark foreboding round the table. There was a too-good looking man with a reserved smile, a fashionable looking man in sunglasses shaking his head to the music, a hard faced woman with blonde hair who seemed to look critically at him, a nervy looking weirdo with a single, rolling bloodshot eye and his own two relatives, neither of whom seemed very familiar at that moment. Everyone sat down, and Chloe loudly finished her sentence: " ... it turned out people like Eliot."

"Eh?" Eliot leaned across the table.

"Elysia. I'm holding you up as an example of why it was abolished."

"Ha ha." Eliot grinned at Maria. "What a card."

"You guys all went to Elysia? That place where the kids disappeared? The Black Dragon?" The Scot said with diffident interest. Then, when no one answered, jocularly: "You mean you're a class enemy, Chlo?" Chloe ignored him.

With a glint in his eye, Eliot said to Chloe: "You shouldn't knock it. The British Empire got started on the playing fields of Elysia Hall." Chloe took the bait: "Yeah! And look what happened to the British Empire!"

Eliot shrugged. "Not my fault if the proles didn't do their bit."

The Scot looked taken aback. Eliot eyed him curiously, then decided there was too much at stake to start a fight. "Only kidding," he laughed. "I never thought much of it myself. Hey Maria, let's go dance." He grabbed her arm and took off.

Chloe turned to Luke and said loudly: "So you still see Eliot?"

"Oh, yeah, yeah; and Martin sometimes."

Chloe looked up. "Really? What's he doing now?"

"He's dealing. Doing quite well out of it, I believe ... doing quite well out of me at any rate."

"Well, well."

"You still see anyone?"

Yes. As it happens, I live with Suzanne."

"*You*, with *Suzanne*?"

"Don't look so surprised. She changed."

"Wow! Elysiolers never part, huh? So ... how is she?"

"She's OK."

Luke wasn't listening. He was remembering; a party. Misted windows. The smell of punch, laughter. When was that good memory from? When was ... and then, like in a dream, just as he was on the verge of it ... it became terrible, a nightmare. He shook it off. It left. Best thing, he decided, shakily swigging his Schlitz.

IX

The bedroom was strangely like a floodlit aquarium. Martin was wondering why and realized that the bright lights of London were reflecting off the river and pulsing through the vast circular window in faint, wavy shadows.

"When I want you," Nadeine said, "it's like every particle of my being desires you. Every inch of it. God, I love it. "

Martin was standing by the window, only half watching her.

"Take off your clothes. No, wait. I want you to watch me."

Nadeine stood up from the bed and with a deft movement sent her shift tumbling in a pile of expensive silk to the ground. She was naked. "Come here. Sit down." She ordered. "Pull up that chair, put it at the end of the bed. " Silently, Martin obeyed. She got back onto the bed and lay down. Her right hand moved slowly across her stomach to the V of her pubic hair. "When I think about you, I feel like it would be better to own you." her fingers spread across the valley of her groin, and her smooth thighs moved apart. "I think of you, and I think of love. I think of ... your hard strong body against me. I think of your tongue ... " the fingers began to work, slowly, up and down, long painted nails glittering against a sudden wetness. "I want you, and I want you so much ... that I am afraid.

Because if I do not own your body, and everything must be owned, then one day it will belong to someone else." She exhaled sharply, and her buttocks moved upwards in a brief movement, like the lap of sea against the shore. "I think of your hardness, and I think of how it feels when it touches me, here ... I think of death, and blood, and something, some spring in me gives ... " The fingers were pressing deep now, the lower part of her body undulating. "I get so close to you, but it's not that close, because one day you might be gone, and ... come here ... come close, but don't touch me ... wait, wait ... " She was silent for several seconds, as her body began to glisten with sweat. Her lips parted, and she bit the lower one. The muscles on her neck and stomach tensed as she bent forward. "Now! Close.. closer ... closer ... wait." Martin leaned forward until he was so close he could feel the heat of her pudenda on his hand. She quivered and let out a groan, her back arched, and froze. Then slowly, very slowly, she relapsed back to the bed. "And you see, if I can't have all of you, always, then I have to wonder ... whether I want you at all."

She opened her eyes. Martin was expressionless.

"We understand each other," she said.

X

"Oh, man! Look what he's doing with that guitar!" the sunglassed man said.

"Like killing a cat," his companion agreed cheerfully. Everyone looked at them curiously for a second.

Suddenly Jason leant across the table towards Luke. Luke saw him coming and looked startled.

"I really digged ... dug your Dad's last film," the red-eyed apparition hissed. "Oh, really?" Luke said, taken aback. "What was that?" There was a pause. Jason's mouth fell open and fluttered like a fish. "I ... I ... can't ... The name ... " Luke felt a moment of deep bonding. He leant over eagerly. "Don't worry," he said hoarsely, "that happens to me too. It's my mind! Completely fucked." The boy gave him a frozen stare. "Anyway," Luke went on hastily, "he doesn't make films. It's arms."

"Eliot ... I thought Eliot said he was a film producer."

"No. Arms."

"*Arms* ?"

"Right. The films launder the cash. He finances them, but he's not really involved. It's arms."

Jason realized, with a horror that made his jaw drop, that he was being made fun of. The weirdo, who had for a moment seemed like a friend, was in with the rest of them. They were all mocking him; soon they would doubtless take him from this club to some quiet alley and beat him to death. They *hate* me! He decided. Their animal instincts were coming out in this ... this bacchanalian dungeon, they were looking for the runt to pick on. All he could hope was that they might forget him if he remained absolutely silent.

* * *

Eliot, on the floor, had just tried to kiss Maria. She had taken off her top and now her breasts were concealed only by the thin cotton of her T-shirt. It had all been too much. But Maria had pushed him away. He wasn't sure why. Nor was she.

"Let's go outside and have some more coke." Eliot suggested on impulse. Maria hesitated ... then nodded, though she knew she was burning her boats. Eliot reached for her hand and pulled her out through the crowd; then he paused and changed direction, back up onto the podium. He went round to Luke, who was mumbling something to Chloe. "Luke." he whispered in his friend's ear. The voice was so hoarse and excited, Luke took it to be the unstable cousin and pulled away. "Luke, come here. Listen. Have you got any H?"

"Heroin? I wish I did. Try Martin."

"No. I need it NOW."

"I've been after it all day. Forget it." Eliot cursed and went away with Maria.

"What's he up to?" Chloe asked.

"I think he's trying to get off with his cousin."

"Isn't that ... ? "

Luke shrugged and shook his head.

"Do you know?" he asked Jason, discovering that he was being stared at again. Jason didn't hear, so he smiled shakily and nodded agreement.

"I've got some H." Chloe said.

* * *

" ... I'm going WAY DOWN SOUTH,
Way down to MEXICO ...
I said MaaaaKKKEEEEEEeeeeekooo ..."

Eliot could hardly believe his luck. He put it down to the booze. As it was, his primary concern was to get on with it before she came out of the coma.

There was a secondary problem too, no less pressing. Where? He had done this once before, with a girl from Stoke Newington whose workday job was wrestling in mud, but her sensibilities had perhaps been less acute than Maria's. He had taken the mud wrestler to the only place there was to take a girl at Camden Lock: under the bridge. Eliot's heart was pumping like a steam shovel as he led her towards the canal. Surely she would blink, snap out of it, slap him and run? But they reached the towpath without incident. Perhaps she didn't realize his intentions, was too innocent? No, even in Broadstairs a girl her age knew that much. Maybe ... Mother of Christ! In the shadows, mumbling, grunting, a couple already there. No, it was worse! A whole orgiastic gang of them ... Couples like flies, writhing up against the cold wall of the railway bridge, among the coke cans and fag packets. He glanced at her. This was the moment of truth.

She looked a little more alert. Nothing else. But had she seen? Must've done by now. Then they entered the shadows, she turned to him, and to his amazement she was pulling him towards her as she backed up against a few square inches of wall, her mouth was reaching for his, her tongue in his mouth, God, he could've laid the lot of them with joy! She *wanted* him!

* * *

Her back against the wall. His body pressing in, smelling of beer and sweat and cigarettes, his strong hands as they felt for her — she gasped, opened her eyes. He was dark, his eyes were closed. She looked to her right. A woman in a kind of Spanish flamenco dress had her breasts spilled out, just feet away. She was on her knees with another woman in jodhpurs, her fingers working through the fly. The second woman was giving head to a man, a man like a dumper truck, a snorting whale of a man. She smiled at Maria. Maria smiled back, panting. Eliot had eased her jeans downwards. God, was this really happening? She felt hot, wanted to scream with excitement, confined herself to a few short gasps. These seemed to spur Eliot on. Long before she expected it, he was suddenly there, the heat of him like a thick fist against her. Then she wanted to laugh as she thought, what if Bill could see her now, pale Bill who she called her boyfriend back in Broadstairs with his dismal pony tail and Ray-Bans. She half giggled, half gasped simultaneously, and caught a glimpse of Eliot's unforgivable grin. Then he was gone, dropping. His tongue, searching, stimulating, her knees felt weak. It didn't last. He was up again, panting for air. His strong arms took her under each leg, hoisted her. She thought of Bill one more time then forgot him. "*Go on!*" she heard herself moan, and was amazed at the words. Eliot needed no encouragement. He positively strode into her, deep, then still deeper, it felt better than she had ever dreamed possible. Somewhere, she saw the two women on her right again. Their eyes had all gone soft and heavy, their mouths were lolling. The man had one hand in each of them. Then they turned and kissed each other. Maria squeezed down, seized by a furious hunger. Eliot, groaning like a wounded soldier, thrust inwards, deeper, deeper, and the motion became harder, hotter, faster. She was lifted up on a wave. She took a deep breath and yelled. His spurt was like molten lava, massaging in, up, through to the pinnacles of her breasts, up her throat. "Oh, Christ!" she shrieked, and saw the two women part and smile at her.

*What the fuck,* she asked herself immediately it was done, *is going on?*

XI

I could have a problem." Martin said quietly. He was again standing by the great round window.

"What kind of a problem?"

"I'm not sure yet."

"Business?"

"Yes." Nadeine took a sip of champagne and levelled her eyes at him. The light in the room was blue from concealed lamps. "Is it going to cause trouble?"

"I don't know. Probably not."

"Then why do I think you're worried?"

"Because it shouldn't have happened."

Nadeine shrugged.

"Listen," Martin said, "I think I'm going to get out of the city for a few days. I need somewhere to stay. How about your place in Sussex?"

"No. My father's there."

"Doesn't he ever go to work?"

"Even MEPs have holidays. Hotel?"

"No. Somewhere private. And I need it now."

"Maybe I could ask some friends. But not 'till morning." Martin nodded.

"Now, will you come to bed?" She placed a slim hand on the pillow and smiled. Martin gazed out at the pyramid of lights still shining in St. Katherine's Dock on the other side of the river. "Either some people never go to bed," he said, "or a lot of people sleep with their lights on." He turned and looked at Nadeine as she crushed her cigarette out.

"Maybe," she said, "they're frightened of the dark."

* * *

HEEEEEEEEEEEEEEEY, Joe,
Where you going to run to now?
I said Heeeeeeeeeeeeey Joe,
Where you going to Ruuuuun to now?

Eliot and Maria returned as the band was playing its final encore. Eliot looked pleased with himself. The Scotsman and Chloe's date were on their feet, finally galvanized by the music. Jason sat with a face like an Easter Island statue. Luke was telling Chloe with unusual animation about the accident he'd had that afternoon, to her amusement.

A few minutes later, they were all outside.

"Right," said the Scot. "I've got to be up early tomorrow; recording session." He looked round at their blank faces, clearly disappointed that none lit up with recognition.

"We'll go back to the flat." Eliot said, his arms round Maria. "You're staying with your father, aren't you?" he added pointedly to Luke. Luke nodded and giggled.

"Well," Chloe turned to the writer. "Your place or mine?" But he coughed nervously. "Oh, no. no. No. I'm with ... " he gestured towards the sun-glassed Scot who smiled uncertainly. A moment later a taxi passed and the two men ran off to catch it.

"Well," said Luke, "you can stay at my place if you want. I don't think I can offer you sex or anything like that, but we could have a good breakfast tomorrow."

After a beat, Chloe laughed uproariously.

"Sounds good to me," she said when she'd recovered.

* * *

Later that night, Martin climbed quietly out of bed, wrapped himself in a silk dressing gown and let himself out of the bedroom. He went down the hall to the private lift which took him to the underground parking. There he retrieved a package from his car, which he stared at for a long time before moving again.

After completing his business in the garage, which took about ten minutes, he silently returned to the flat. From the lift he went upstairs into the living room. Already the air was unpleasantly stale, the toll of cigarettes and bleary drunken breath. There was a litter of champagne bottles and ashtrays around the floor. He wandered to the dining table where they had eaten, and examined a wrought iron candelabra. Next he turned to a slim, minutely decorated Japanese vase on a table by the wall. He examined this too.

He then turned out all the lights in the room, and returned to the vase. Fifteen minutes later, he was back in bed.

## XII

Luke woke sweating, and was surprised to find that he was not alone under the heavy duvet. At first he thought Chloe was awake, dozing, but after a minute of staring at her half-open mouth and the tiny bead of spittle at its lower corner, he realized she was deep asleep. With a sudden flush of nerves, he realized what he could do. A minute later, his hand crept stealthily towards her. He touched her arm, softly, and felt a flutter in his groin. He blushed as his fingers brushed their way up the arm then as they reached the middle of her biceps dropped to the soft mound of her bosom. His fingers stroked the warm skin, swept lower, and with a great well of excitement, came up against the soft swelling of her nipple. His free hand reached between his legs. A minute later, he had acquired the courage to go beyond; his hand quivered south. Her thigh was so hot, and in the crevice between her legs ... "Luke, if you want it, you can have it."

Luke's hand moved away faster than from a hot oven. "No, no ... " He managed to mumble.

"She moved, nimbly, and got his hand before he could get out of range. "Why not," she said. Luke was horrified. "Can't!" he gasped, with the conviction of honesty. Chloe thought about it.

"Hand then. Come on, I'll do you too." She thrust his trembling hand down before he could protest. It seemed to get caught, like in a trap. "No!" he yelped, pulling away. "I really can't." Chloe laughed and rolled over. "Only kidding, Luke."

Luke decided to take no chances. He got up quickly, put on a dressing gown and went downstairs to the kitchen. It was, he saw by the electric clock on the wall, only eight-thirty. There was no sign of Dorothy. He was still shaking.

He made some coffee, managing to remember where it was kept from when he had lived here permanently.

Taking the coffee upstairs on a tray, he considered the situation. Chloe in his bed. The first time he had shared a bed for weeks, maybe months. And Chloe, of all people ... entering the bedroom, he surmised that she had gone back to sleep. He put the tray on a table before climbing under the duvet.

Chloe. That was particularly odd in as much as he actually knew her. Had known her for ages. Not that they'd been friends at school, but he knew most of what there was to know about her — or would have done if he could remember ... it was strange, but that period more than any other was a real black hole. Elysia. Things had been different then, for sure. There was something ... something about Chloe, which he'd almost remembered last night ... what was that?

Chloe rolled over onto her stomach and began to prop herself up on her elbows, looking round. The first look she gave him could have been umbrage, or simply non-recognition. Luke yawned to cover his embarrassment.

"I smell coffee." She told him.

Luke reached over and passed her the second mug. Out of the corner of his eye he watched her take a sip, holding the mug with both hands.

"Good," she said, and put the mug down. Then she shifted onto her back, propping the pillows up behind her. Luke observed the roll of her breasts with covert interest.

Chloe grunted and asked what time it was. Luke told her.

"Is the sun shining?"

"Yes."

"Pity. Sun and London ... nightmare."

There was a long pause. Luke's ears hummed with the silence.

"What do you these days?" he asked after a moment, deferentially.

"Nothing." There was another long silence, then she sighed heavily and recited, "I finished college last summer, my old man got me a job at his bank. I dropped a lot in my first month though, so it didn't last. Met Suzanne and moved in with her a few months ago. And ... some bloke who fancies me wants to make a TV play out of a short story I wrote. That's it."

"What's the story about?"

"Fucking. At Cambridge."

"Sounds good." Luke quickly changed the subject. "And ... you and Suzanne are friends now?"

"I wouldn't say that." Chloe obviously didn't like the question. She asked: "And you?"

"Oh, nothing ... I mean *really* nothing."

"Good for you." Chloe said. Luke muttered something inaudible.

"What?" Chloe said.

"I just said it's Saturday. Weekend. Another one."

Then the phone rang. Luke picked up the receiver and said: "Martin!" in a surprised voice.

XIII

Martin had awoken late and found Nadeine already gone. All that remained was her morning mirror on the bedside table, one white line still on it and a note underneath. Martin detached the note. It read: "I have just called Marie-Louise (Perroux) (Do you remember her?) and she says her parents will let you use their "gatehouse". It's a very nice cottage actually and you can have it as long as you want. Address as below, ask in the village if you get lost. Take care. Call me soon." Nadeine had signed it and beneath was a Wiltshire address. Martin got up and dressed.

In the kitchen he made himself coffee and put bread in the toaster. The flat was quiet, though he assumed there were still people sleeping in the other bedrooms. Checking his watch, he saw that it was still only nine o'clock. He picked up the phone and dialled a number in Nassau. It rang three times, then was answered.

"Pascual."

"Martin here. Sorry about the time, but it's urgent. Is Alex around?"

"No."

"Will he be in?"

"No."

"Well… can I leave a message?"

"If you want."

"Thanks. Pascual, is something going on? Something you'd like to share with me?"

"No."

"Well, please tell Alex, tell him, I'm having some trouble with our tame policeman Walters. He won't answer the phone, and I think he may have thrown me out. The police were waiting for me at a drop last night. Got that?" There was silence.

Martin rang off.

Next he rang Luke's flat in Redcliffe Square. The phone was answered after half a minute by Eliot who told him to try Hampstead, which he did.

"Luke ... "

\* \* \*

"Martin!"

"Did I wake you?"

Luke made an expansive denial which Martin interrupted by clearing his throat. "Luke ... I've got to get away for a few days. It's a bit urgent. I was wondering if there was any chance I could use the Millhouse."

"The Millhouse?"

"Yes. Dorset. If your Dad still owns it."

"Yeah ... I guess he does ... "

"Well, can I stay there for the weekend? It'll just be me. Could you ask your father?"

"Dad's away, but you can use it, sure."

"Thanks, Luke. Are the keys still in the same place?"

"I suppose so."

"I appreciate this, Luke. I really do." Before Luke had a chance to ask any questions, Martin had put the phone down.

\* \* \*

He made three further calls. To each person he gave the information that he wouldn't be taking calls as he was going away. But he would be in touch within the week. There was no problem with supply, he didn't expect any delays. None of his correspondents seemed too bothered by the news and no one asked any questions.

Finally, he copied the information from Nadeine's note onto a piece of paper which he placed in his wallet, and wrote on the original note: "I'll be there." before leaving it under the coffee jug.

* * *

"That was Martin." Luke said.

"I heard."

"He's going to the Millhouse for the weekend. You remember the Millhouse?"

Luke pursed his lips and thought for a while. Chloe smoked with her eyes closed.

"Chloe ... " Luke said to the inert figure beside him. "I've had an idea. I think I might go down and join him. Get some air — you know. Would you ... like to come?"

"Well, Luke, that's a very interesting idea. And how about if I call Suzanne? If Martin is going down, that should interest her. Then we could all go, make it a party."

"Right! More the merrier. I can call Eliot too."

"*Eliot?*"

"Yeah. He's my best friend."

# XIV

The sky, which had been brilliant blue in Hampstead and all the way through London to Richmond, had now turned a mottled and ominous grey, the colour of week-old city snow.

There was little conversation in Luke's father's blue Lexus as it swept south-west along the M3. Everyone except Eliot, who was driving, was asleep. Luke was in the passenger seat, Chloe, Suzanne and Maria were in the back.

Eliot, in fact, had been rather delighted by the turn of events; one reason was Jason's note, discovered when he'd got up for water. "Sorry," it read. "Just remembered that I have to be in Broadstairs in morning, very important. Thanks for every." The word *very* was heavily underscored.

Whilst getting rid of Jason had been Eliot's exact intention, he found now that it presented unforeseen problems. Jason might be in such a state that he would go home and tell his mother everything; and even more importantly, the source of the money had just dried up. Luke's invitation was a simple way to make both these problems disappear.

Anyway, he was far from averse to spending a weekend with women like Suzanne and Chloe. On Luke's instructions he asked Maria if she would like to come too. He hadn't expected her prompt agreement, in fact he had been surprised enough not to find her snivelling with remorse that morning.

"I've just finished my exams." Maria had said with faint irritation, catching his look. "I've got a right to do something on my own now, haven't I?" Eliot wasn't arguing.

\* \* \*

Shortly after leaving the motorway, Eliot discovered that he was lost and that there were no maps in the car. Since they were on open road and there was no one around to ask for directions, the only option was to drive on.

But the four-lane A road dissolved into a wide two-laner, then became narrower and began to look patchy and uncared for.

Although it wasn't actually raining, the weather was peculiar and the country had recently been drenched. Vast black clouds scudded across an otherwise sharp blue sky, leaving gaps where great shafts of sunbeam penetrated then instantly dissolved.

From a criss-cross landscape of patchwork fields, the road descended into a long stretch of woodland and then emerged into an odd, arrow straight avenue lined with tall conifers that reminded Eliot of some holiday in France; there was no other traffic, and he began to get nervous.

Luke woke, rolled a joint, and admitted that he had no idea where they were. He smoked and passed the joint to Eliot then closed his eyes again. Eliot drove too fast and began to mutter.

After they had been on the road for two hours and lost for twenty minutes, an air of restlessness grew in the car as the others awoke. Chloe said: "You'll just have to stop and knock on someone's door." Eliot pointed out impatiently that there were no doors. Chloe tutted irritably.

Then, leaving a valley and entering a long, flat plain, they came quite suddenly upon "Maybelline's Cafe and Truckstop". Eliot pulled into the muddy parking lot and turned the motor off.

The cafe, a faded pink, single storey building on short brick stilts, stood in the middle of moist, ochre fields. Smoke rose from a single chimney. It was caught in the beam of a long shaft of light, and its shabbiness was accentuated. There were three other vehicles in the car park; two middle-weight trucks and an orange Beetle with a broken rear-quarter window.

"Let's eat." Eliot said. No one showed enthusiasm, but one by one they climbed out of the car.

The smell inside the cafe was sweet and overfamiliar, bread and jam, grease and tea. The two truckers were sitting at separate but identical tables by the windows. One was reading the Mirror, the other, older, wearing a proper shirt, not a T-shirt, stared at them as they filed in. An early Led Zeppelin song was playing incongruously on the jukebox. Maybelline, if she was there at all, was not behind the small cluttered counter. Eliot led the way to a booth. They squeezed in and passed the typewritten menu round.

Eliot was opposite Chloe. She was looking very good, he decided. He hadn't been able to get a decent look under the lights at Dingwalls, but now he could see she was fresh and ... peachlike. Sexy as hell, in fact, with that permanent sneer — or at least, the sneer she permanently looked at him with. Fancy her sleeping with Luke. He himself had kissed her once, that was right, then something odd had happened ...

Suddenly Suzanne got up and he switched his attention to her. Still classy too, he decided, but not taking such good care of herself, which was a shame. He turned back to Chloe. That kiss ... it had been in the Millhouse too ... a good omen? Who was it? ... Charlie ... Oh shit, kill *that* memory.

At that moment Chloe too got up and squeezed out. The younger trucker stared at her as she followed Suzanne to the ladies'. As she passed him he said something. She held his eye, leaned forward and muttered in his face. Eliot saw the trucker shrivel and grinned. A class piece, Chloe.

\* \* \*

Inside the tiny, hospital-green painted bathroom, Suzanne was leaning over a sink beneath a cracked mirror. As Chloe entered she saw her flatmate throw back her head and slap her hand to her mouth. Chloe stood still, noticing the smell of Lavender. Suzanne turned to her and smiled, wiping the back of her hand on her mouth. The syringe was in her hand.

There was a pause.

"Martin's coming." Chloe said in the silence. And added stonily: "I meant to tell you." For a second neither of them moved. An expresso machine gurgled quietly beyond the plaster wall.

Deliberately, Suzanne injected herself, wiped the syringe on a tissue, replaced its cap from the sink, and put it in her bag.

"Why didn't you?"

Chloe didn't answer.

Suzanne sighed. "The Chemist's son."

"What?"

"The Chemist's son."

"*What?*"

"His only son. Didn't you know?"

"Suzanne, he's coming."

"Well," Suzanne said slowly, "these days I rather like chemistry."

Chloe felt herself grow angry. She hated it when Suzanne played this game, but was too afraid to say so. She scowled instead, and started to say something. Suzanne cut her short.

"It doesn't matter Chloe. In fact, I thought he might turn up. I ... kind of felt it ... Something happened last night. It's appropriate." Suzanne shook her head, her eyes were black and empty.

* * *

A woman of forty came out of a door behind the counter wearing Scholl sandals and an acrylic dress the same colour as the building. She exchanged her cigarette for a note pad, came sluggishly over to their table and nodded.

Everyone wanted scrambled eggs, so they ordered them for Chloe and Suzanne too.

"Paper?" The woman asked.

"FT please." Eliot said sarcastically.

"Sun or Mirror."

"The Sun will do nicely."

The Led Zeppelin song on the jukebox came to an end with a jarring guitar chord. Luke looked thoughtful and said: "Mmmm. Quite good, really." Suzanne came out, intercepted Maybelline and said brusquely: "Did they order? I just want tea." Maybelline went on out the back, probably, as Eliot observed, to spit in their eggs.

Back in the car, Luke swapped places with Chloe. Eliot followed the directions Maybelline had grudgingly given them. From her they knew that they had wandered off course onto Salisbury Plain. But it was not far back to the main road, which would lead them to where they were going. Soon the roads widened and other traffic joined them.

"You think that place was real?" Luke asked at one point. The others looked at him but no one answered.

At a little before two, under a mottled, uncertain sky, Eliot turned off a B road into a lane. It ran down a gentle chalky slope through green fields to the banks of the river and the Millhouse: a black and white half-timbered Tudor mansion.

## XV

From the head of the lane it was possible to see a tiny village further down the valley. It disappeared from sight as the track descended. From the Millhouse itself, no other sign of human life was visible.

Eliot pulled the Lexus up in the cobbled courtyard and turned the engine off. For a moment the only sound was the motion of the river a few yards away.

"Peace." Eliot said at last, first to be embarrassed by the quiet. Luke opened his door. "Looks like we got here before Martin," he said. Still no one moved.

"Well," Eliot said, "are you coming, or what?"

Lethargically, everyone climbed out of the car. Luke went away to find the keys, Eliot stretched and looked around. Looking away from the buildings the view was a picture-book scene; fields, the river with a small wooden footbridge fording it, and the great swathe of forest stretching down the valley towards hills.

"Hasn't changed," Eliot said, "has it?"

Chloe, who was nearest to him, said irritably "What did you expect? A shopping mall?" Eliot grinned after her as she started towards the river.

Maria said to Suzanne, who was leaning against the car with her hands in her pockets and her head down: "Do you come here often?" Suzanne appeared not to hear. Eliot answered. "Not at all." He felt self-conscious, and cleared his throat. "I haven't been down here for years. Not since we were at school together."

"Elysia."

"Yeah. It's on the other side of those woods." He pointed at the hills. "We had some fun. Weekends and things, we could say we were spending the night with our parents or make some excuse, and come here instead. We had some good times. While it lasted."

"What happened?"

"Oh ... " Eliot glanced at Chloe, but she had her back to him. "It just ended."

Maria went to peer through a window. "Wow!" she said. "What a kitchen!"

Luke returned and unlocked the front door. It opened onto a stone-floored hallway, with an ancient wooden staircase rising at the rear. The tick of a mahogany-cased grandfather clock was the only sound.

"Come on, then," Luke said, stepping across the threshold. Maria followed, but Eliot hung back, suddenly thinking about why the fun had ended. "Move!" Chloe groaned behind him and gave him a push. He was pleased by her touch and put the bad thought away.

"This is fabulous," Maria said, glancing through open doors.

"Wait 'till you see the bedrooms." Eliot said. "The master has mirrors ... " It started jauntily, but his voice faded somewhat on the last syllable. Behind him he heard Chloe snort. *She remembers,* he thought.

Luke headed for the kitchen. He sat down at the heavy wooden table with a sigh and began to roll himself a joint. "If you're going to look round, you might just stop by the cellar." He called out to Eliot. Eliot shouted back with a hint of effort: "This is going to be a good weekend, Luke. I can feel it in my bones!"

XVI

Martin crossed the river by London Bridge and was in Upper Street within minutes. Instead of cutting across to Gibson Square along Theberton Street as usual, he parked a little further north in Barnsbury Street.

Now he called his home phone number from the car phone, and was greeted by the answering-machine message he'd left the previous evening. After listening to it he hung up. He was about to get out of the car when he hesitated and picked up the car phone again. He called the number of the people who lived below him, which he had obtained from directory enquiries some time ago. After ringing five times, the receiver was lifted. Martin adjusted his voice. "Good morning, Mr, ah, Richards? This is Sergeant Dole, calling from the Upper Street Police Station. I just want to check that you've been informed of the police operation we're mounting in your area." The phone expressed a muffled negative. Martin felt for the ignition keys, and affected surprise. "No? Well, you may have noticed some activity around your building?"

"I've heard some banging upstairs if that's what you mean." Martin's hand froze. The fear was like waking to find himself on a narrow girder hundreds of feet above the ground and somehow *knowing* he was about to fall. "Yes. I hope you weren't disturbed?"

"No, no. I just noticed them this morning ... I thought the chap upstairs had visitors, but ... "

"That's right sir." Martin kept his voice steady. "Well, not to worry. Someone come in and explain it all. Thank you, and goodbye."

Martin put the phone down.

The fear made him want to groan. He could feel his face grow white with it. He tried to breathe slowly, to swallow. It was impossible to believe that it would go away. In fact it lasted for about thirty seconds. Then it disappeared.

After a moment of sitting quite still, he started the engine and set off towards Knightsbridge and his safety deposit bank. There he collected money and a false passport.

After that he drove to Heathrow, and had almost reached the Swissair desk before he felt strong enough to change his mind.

# XVII

"Luke. Hey, Luke ... " It was Eliot, shaking him roughly by the shoulder and talking loudly.

"Jesus, Eliot." Luke said.

"Sorry, man. You were asleep."

"I noticed." He was on-bed, fully clothed, in his bedroom on the first floor. Behind Eliot, Maria stood quietly. Eliot parked himself on the bed beside Luke without invitation. "Everything's looking good." Eliot's full good cheer was restored. "I turned the water on in the pool, we've got electric light and gas. Only one problem." Eliot waited expectantly.

"What's that?"

"No food."

"Oh."

"But don't panic. I'll drive into town and get some."

"That's great. Appreciate it." Luke shut his eyes again.

"Only thing, Luke ... we need some moulin. I'm a little short at the moment ... " Luke fished his wallet out of his back pocket and threw it to Eliot without opening his eyes.

"Use the card." He grunted.

"The good Lord loves you, babe, and will reward you. In fact, I will reward you, just as soon as ... "

"OK, great."

"See you later then."

"Great."

Once Eliot was gone, Luke found that he couldn't get back to sleep though he still felt tired. The lump on his head had begun to ache again, and he thought he should fetch aspirin. He opened his eyes and rolled from side to side, staring at the walls of his bedroom. Old posters, he'd been meaning to take them down for years. Ripped in the corners. The Rolling Stones poster from "Emotional Rescue", and the Clash one from "Combat Rock". Three big Van Gogh prints from a school trip to Amsterdam years ago. He didn't even like them much now, but at least they were familiar. What else? Red wooden desk, with an old manual typewriter on it. Bookcase with a few books, mostly children's, he hadn't read so much recently. His head really hurt. A cardboard box by the wall containing a lot of Tintins. He looked again at the typewriter. Where had he got that? He couldn't remember. Why did he have it then? Because he'd once written things on it ... almost before the thought was fully formed, he recalled something. He rolled off the bed, ignoring the thudding in his skull, and started rooting through the box. After a while he found "The Red Sea Sharks", and the papers inside it. He pulled one out. It was badly typewritten. He grinned as he began to read it:

> His eyes are eyes which speak to me,
> Of things beyond the ken of mortals.
> Betwixt a world of sweetness hidden
> and the useless, worthless world,
> A book of life in a dungeon of hell,

A hope foretold, a promise promised.
These eyes are Charlie's eyes.

Luke's grin slowly faded, and he stared at it until his eyes watered.

## XVIII

Chloe went out through the hall, stopping for a moment to pick up a white mac which she put round her shoulders. She was feeling strangely abrasive, had been since they'd entered the house. As soon as she stepped outside she felt the drizzle in the air, the clouds having gathered overhead again.

The garden leading towards the woods was narrow but well kept. Someone was mowing the lawns regularly and there were even rudimentary flowerbeds. On one side was the river, on the other a ditch and wooden fence to keep the cows in the next field out. Beyond lay a thick expanse of woodland, stretching away in a crescent that followed the river's course along the valley.

She walked slowly to the end of the garden, turning once to watch the car with Eliot and Maria pull away with a growl and a squeak on the cobbles as Eliot pressed the accelerator too hard. This irritated her, for no particular reason.

The ditch swung hard across the garden at its furthest point before joining the river. The "bridge" was still there, all three planks of it and no more appreciably rotted or decayed than five, or was it six, years ago, when she'd last been here. She tested one of the planks with her foot and it was firm. She hesitated and turned back to the house for a moment. There was no sign of life there. She ran her tongue along her upper teeth, and stepped forward.

A second later she was across. It was soggily wet underfoot and muddy where cows, sheltering under the nearest trees, had sunk into the soft clay. She wondered for a second whether her hi-tops would be waterproof. Probably not, she decided. But she wanted to go on.

It tended to be drier near the foot of the trees, and by hopping and skipping she made her way along. The brush became thicker, then she crossed a stile and found a vague path leading into the dim, wet wedge of forest. She followed it in.

At once she remembered, and was struck by, the sweet smell of decay that permeated the rotting undergrowth of broken branches, furze, brambles, the whole deep floor of claustrophobic mess. A few birds twittered forlornly, the drizzle hissed, but otherwise it was silent. She looked up. Few chinks of light penetrated.

She moved on, pushing through a thick growth of grass that overhung the dwindling path. After a minute or two she began to feel tired, soporific. It was like being in a stomach, she thought suddenly, a digestible item waiting for the gastric juices.

The path died, and she discovered that she was lost and going nowhere. But with irritation overcoming a start of alarm, she went on. She was feeling faintly apprehensive, and deliberately avoided thinking about where she was going.

After about fifteen minutes she found it. There was what amounted to a clearing, though it was just a few square yards. In its centre stood a squat stone shed, perhaps six by eight feet, the height of a tall man. It was old, perhaps ancient, and the stone and concrete had crumbled on the left side facing her. The roof too was gone. Apart from a doorway without a door, a hole for a window to one side of it, and the fact that there was a floor of sorts under a layer of mud, it was just a haphazard pile of stones. Chloe stood quietly before it, shivering slightly in the drizzle.

For a long time she simply stared. Finally she stepped towards the door.

The shed smelt. Otherwise it was as she recalled. She knew exactly which part of the wall to look for and turned to it accordingly. But there was nothing there. Surprised, she approached the wall to the right of the door and looked more carefully, scanning the stonework. But there was still no sign of what she wanted. Then she realized. The rain and time and dust had totally obscured it. With the palm of her hand she rubbed against the stone and a coat of muddy slime came away. She picked up a handful of wet leaves from the ground and rubbed again. When the stone was fully exposed, the writing, roughly hewn with a sharp pebble became visible. It read, "Chlo and Charlie this way come on" beyond which an outsize exclamation mark had been carved. Chloe stared at it, smiled, and frowned. Water splashed against her cheek and eyelid from an overhanging branch, and she blinked.

"Fucking joke." She whispered out loud, doubtfully.

## XIX

*Carlito, aka Charlie, di Angelis was indisputably Italian, from his long, aquiline nose to the tips of his perfect Gucci loafers. His father was said to be a Tuscan nobleman down on his luck, and for this reason, the myth ran, Charlie tended to wear somewhat old-fashioned clothes. Of the highest possible quality, certainly, but slightly threadbare: hand-me-downs. It was a suggestion which added to his already romantic image.*

*He was right behind Chloe when she came to an abrupt halt.*

*"Jesus!" he exclaimed, exaggerating his Italian accent. "What's that?"*

*"It's what we, in English, call a shed, or a hut ... or a shack ... "*

*"So we're lost, Chlo-Chlo."*

*Chloe turned. Some of Charlie's long brown hair had slipped forward, masking his smoothly tanned face. He was grinning lopsidedly.*

*"You look like a sheepdog. A drunk sheepdog." Chloe said. Charlie raised his arms. In one hand he carried a day-glo pink monkey, in the other a half bottle of rum. He took a swig from the bottle, gasped, wiped his mouth with the monkey and said: "I may be drunk, but at least I don't lead people into the middle of bogs calling it a short cut!"*

*Chloe cut in impatiently, saying: "It's not a bog."*

*"It's mud, isn't it?"*

"It's not a bog." Chloe repeated. "It's a wood. Bogs do not occur in woods."

"Well, it's a wood with mud in it and that's bad enough." Chloe rolled her eyes, but he could tell she was enjoying it.

"I wish you'd ... dispose of that monkey," she said meaningfully. There was a moment's silence, then they both laughed.

"It's my prize!" Charlie protested.

"You mean you almost shot the guy's head off. He only gave it you so you'd go away."

"Well," Charlie shrugged, "I tell you what. I'll give it to you. It means a lot to me, but ... here."

He extended his arm, holding the monkey out. Chloe hesitated, then took it and tried to rip its head off. Charlie rushed to its defence, and they spent the next minute struggling together at the foot of a birch. The struggle ended abruptly when Charlie realized he was virtually hugging her.

He hesitated. She leant toward him, willing his compliance. But he suddenly seemed shy and pulled away.

A less determined person than Chloe might have been put off. "Charlie," she whispered. "Kiss me." And promptly kissed him.

It seemed to work. He fell into the kiss, eyes tightly shut, while she watched him and gauged him like a technician with an experiment in hand. She gave him a few seconds, then began to worry that the hand on her arm was not moving much — and definitely not to her breast. She gave him a few more seconds, then artfully twisted, moaning almost inaudibly, so that his hand either went with her arm or slid round ... and it worked. As soon as his hand touched the rich, warm wool of her sweater there, the magic took place. The movement of his tongue became urgent. With a murmur of pleasure, she pressed back.

But Chloe knew her man and was already one step ahead. Suddenly, she pulled away. "I only do this," she whispered, "because I like you so much." These sensitive boys were temperamental. Allow them to go too far too soon, without gaining their confidence first, they would shy at the gate.

*They were still entangled. Chloe met his eyes. Charlie looked away somewhat sheepishly. She straightened and said: "I'm dying of thirst. Pass the bottle, will you." Charlie did as he was told, and Chloe drank. Out of the corner of her eye she saw his adam's apple jumping wretchedly and was pleased.*

*Suddenly he said with nervy belligerence: "But what the hell is that thing?"*

*Chloe stopped drinking and gazed where he was staring and over-emphatically craning his neck. He meant the little hut.*

*"Well, it's not the Millhouse, that's for sure," she said.*

*Charlie strode towards it. "Come on," he said. "Let's go look."*

*"You go." Chloe said. She leaned back against the tree and closed her eyes.*

*The image that formed in her mind was that of Charlie's body, which she'd seen earlier that week at the swimming tournament, as brown and perfect as she'd expected. And he'd won his race.*

*She opened them again and Charlie was nowhere to be seen. Frowning, she pushed herself away from the tree and wandered over to the grey shed.*

*Charlie was inside, or rather, between the roofless walls, a sharp pebble in one hand, which he was scratching against a wall.*

*"This is going to take all bloody day." He complained when he saw her. Chloe looked more closely.*

*"It's going to be "Chloe and Charlie this way come, on their way to have some fun ... " he announced.*

*Chloe put her hand to her mouth and widened her eyes. "Charlie!" she said breathlessly, "A poet!"*

*Charlie dropped his pebble, squeezed his lips together and said: "Right, that's it." Chloe ran out, with Charlie shouting as he followed. A few minutes later they stumbled out of the woods arm in arm and almost fell into a ditch. From there they could see the Millhouse, glistening in the early evening sunlight at the end of a neatly manicured lawn.*

# XX

Chloe had left a cashmere Mao cap in the car which Eliot had persuaded his cousin to wear. With that and her tunic buttoned up to the chin, he thought, she looked like, what was it? One of those page-boy things. In*credibly* sexy with her blonde hair peeking out. Beautiful eyes too. Clear, innocent, blue eyes. God, was he on a roll or what?

They were walking down the High Street, among housewives and retired couples. No one paid them any attention, no one knew how happy Eliot was.

"So," he said chattily, "are you, like, looking forward to going back to school?"

"Should I?"

Eliot was in too good a mood to say bad things about anything, even school. "Sure. Why not?"

"My parents are sending me to a public school for Sixth form. I have this idea of public schools as pretty ... unpleasant places. Old-fashioned."

Eliot waved his arm breezily. "Oh sure. But you make what you can of it."

"And Elysia?"

"Elysia what?"

"Was it like that?"

"Naaah. We were *progressive*." He reflected a moment before adding, "I made some good friends at Elysia."

"That's important."

"No question." Eliot pulled Luke's wallet out and waved it in front of her. She didn't laugh.

"What?"

She sighed and looked serious. "You know, just then, I had a really weird thought." She glanced at him doubtfully. He smiled his encouraging smile.

"Eliot, I've always done pretty well at school."

"I know. That's great."

"My Dad makes these jokes about my becoming a lawyer so as to help with his business."

"Yeah. Uncle John's a great guy." Eliot almost meant it.

"It always seemed, more or less, to make sense. But ... something's like, I feel, changed ... so that I'm ... " She stopped on the pavement and looked into a shop window. "I *think* something's changed very suddenly, and now, I'm not sure."

Eliot, behind her, put his chin on the top of her Mao cap, and stared at their reflection in the glass. "Baby," he said, "something did happen: you met me."

She stared into his reflected eyes. "I know Eliot, but that's not exactly what I mean." Eliot was too suffused with love to hear.

They started off again. "Well, you had a good time at Elysia didn't you?" she asked. Eliot was delighted. Now was the time to tell her about the rich and influential friends he'd made.

And yet, he was reluctant to lie to her. He hadn't so far, other than the big first lie about his job, which had been for Jason's benefit anyway. What if he didn't *need* to? What if she really ... *liked him for himself*, the way things had once been with girls before, in the distant past? With a start he considered telling her the whole truth: a bed-sit on the Edgeware Road living on income support supplemented by bi-weekly visits to a sperm clinic in Victoria. Sassooning, the regulars called it. It was a new and startling thought.

He compromised. "Actually ... I don't often see people from those days. This — with Chloe and Suzanne — is quite unusual. In fact, it's a bit weird." He frowned. "Luke I see a lot of, and Martin, he's supposed to be coming down, so you'll probably see him." He was beginning to lie again. He only saw Martin if he happened to be with Luke when he made a purchase ... irritated, he bit his tongue.

They stopped at a cashpoint and Eliot took out the maximum allowed.

"Right," he said briskly. "There's a Waitrose around here if I remember right."

Maria lapsed into silence and walked with him through the old town to a cleared lot boasting a cadaverous grey shopping complex. Then, to his surprise, she took his arm and said, "Let's not go in there. I saw a proper fishmonger's a little way back. And we'll find a grocer's." Eliot looked down, pleased at her movement, doubtful of her suggestion.

"We weren't really planning to cook anything." he said. Maria laughed and squeezed his arm as though he had just made a joke. "Oh, *I* can cook," she said. And then added, in a dry tone which meant nothing to Eliot: "I know how to do all the right things."

They passed a grocery first and bought quantities of vegetables. At the fishmonger they bought a side of salmon, some dorade, and squid. As Eliot was walking out she called him back. "Eliot. How long do you think we'll be staying?"

Eliot shrugged. "When do you have to get back?"

"No particular time. But I'm wondering whether to buy this monkfish or not — and there's no point unless we're staying here late on Sunday." She frowned. "It's almost a shame not to. It looks fresh, and you don't often see it." Eliot returned to the counter and met the eyes of a huge and very wicked looking fish on a slab consisting, as far as he could see, mainly of teeth in a head.

"A what?" he asked.

"It's a monkfish. But fishermen sometimes call it the devil's fish.

Confusing, isn't it?"

"Yeah. How come?"

Maria smiled. "Well, according to my mum, it's a fish that lives so deep in the sea that for hundreds of years the fishermen only caught glimpses of it, they didn't really know what it looked like. So being optimistic, as people are, they decided to call it the monk fish; then they actually pulled one up and they saw ... this. Hence, the devil's fish." Eliot tore his gaze away from the cruel and bulbous eyes of the dead beast. "Buy it," he said carelessly. "Come on ... I want to show you a pub I used to get drunk at."

"Now, the beauty of this pub," Eliot explained from the lounge bar of the White Horse, "Is the fact that it's got two doors: front and back. And if you sat over ... there;" he pointed towards a shady area at the back of the room, "Then you could keep an eye on the front door and if anyone came in, a teacher or whatever, you could get out the back almost a hundred per cent without being seen."

"And what if the teacher came through the back door?"

"Ah, well, that's the sly part. Look, I'll show you. Come on."

He led her over towards the wall. The tables were set cubicle-ways with high backs to the pew-like benches. A velvet drape hung between the edge of the cubicles and what was apparently the wall. "Now, if you're sitting here ... " Eliot demonstrated, " ... you can see the front door, right, and the back door is right behind you, but you can see a reflection of it in the glass of that mirror. OK. Now, someone comes in; here, sit next to me here." Maria joined him in the cubicle. "Now, shut your eyes and count to three." Maria, sitting beside him, obeyed. There was a rustling as Eliot moved beside her. When she opened her eyes, he was gone. Eliot lifted the curtain, and was revealed. But his head was now at her knee height, and he was beaming. "See," he said, "it's like a secret passage. You just slide out of sight before anyone sees you, and walk round the side here to the door. A doddle, much used in my youth."

"Very good." Maria applauded. Eliot disappeared and came back on the other side to take his seat. "In fact ... I discovered it myself."

"Amazing ... "

Eliot, a little out of breath from his exertions, took a long pull on his drink. "Only problem, of course," he added thoughtfully, "beer here still tastes like pig's piss."

There was a long pause. After his exertions, Eliot was uncharacteristically short of something to say. He heard a sniffle and turned to see what Maria was doing. To his great surprise, she giggled. And then, inexplicably, burst into a peal of laughter. Eliot began to smile, then stopped, uncertain. "What?" he said when she had recovered a little, smiling with her. "Nothing ... " she said. "It's just ... with your head under that curtain ... grinning ... Eliot, did you ever watch Sesame Street?"

"Yes." Eliot said doubtfully.

"Because you looked just like ... like ... " She could hardly get the words out. Eliot was torn between a desire to laugh with her and a certain inquietude.

"Like ... the COOKIE MONSTER!" she shrieked.

XXI

Towards three o'clock Luke sat up and rubbed his eyes. Then with a yawn he made for the bathroom and took a shower. He dressed again in his room, pulling on an old pair of jeans and a red cardigan from the cupboard. After a while he flicked through the collection of LP's lying against the wall, grunting with amusement. But when he went downstairs he took a handful under his arm.

He went first to the kitchen. No one was there; but there was a selection of spirits and wines on the table. Eliot's work, he presumed. He picked up the Old Holborn tin which contained his drug-making apparatus and went through the ground floor looking for people. The whole building was silent, including the main living room where he almost didn't see Suzanne sitting immobile in a high-backed armchair. She had changed into an Aran sweater which she wore over a yellow and black tracksuit. Her feet were bare and she wore sunglasses.

By her arm was a tray with a large earthenware tea pot, a mug, a salt cellar, a glass and a bottle of tequila. The level of the tequila, Luke noticed, had almost reached the label.

"Hello." Luke greeted her, glad not to find himself alone. "I thought everyone had disappeared."

Suzanne looked up slowly.

"No. Chloe went out for a walk, the other two went shopping." Her voice was slightly slurred, and something else Luke could not identify. Edgy.

"Oh."

But then she said: "Would you like some tea?" and indicated the big brown pot beside her. "There's plenty."

"Yeah. Thanks. I'll just get a mug." Luke put his records down and went back into the kitchen. "Seems a bit more friendly," he thought to himself, searching for a cup. If she was drunk, there was more chance of handling her anyway. In that field he had experience. Surprising, though, Suzanne; he didn't remember her being a lush.

Along with the mug he took a glass and a bottle of Scotch back into the living room. "Thought we might get the evening off to a good start," he said apologetically as Suzanne roused herself to pour the tea. She looked at him sharply for a moment. Luke took the sofa and a book from a nearby bookcase and set about rolling a joint on it.

"You're a model now, aren't you?" he asked through the stillness. "I saw you on TV a while back — something for perfume or hairgel; or something. In a desert."

"Moisturizer."

"Right. I guess that must be fun?"

"It's a way of being able to say I do something."

"I know what you mean." Luke nodded thoughtfully. "I sometimes tell people I do all kinds of weird things just to get them off my back. I told a man in a pub the other day that I was a lumberjack. I think he believed me."

Suzanne smiled thinly. Encouraged, Luke decided to attempt a question.

"So, have you done that long, or did you go to college?"

"I went to art school for a year, then dropped out."

"How come?"

"I wasn't getting anywhere."

"Uh huh."

They sat in silence for a while as Luke fashioned the joint into a neat cone.

"I didn't go to college ... " he said reflectively, and frowned. "I didn't go to college at all, and if you ask me, I didn't miss much. I mean, you meet some of these students, they just make you sick, they don't know *anything*! I mean, they really don't. Not a fucking clue. Oh, I mean, they may know about eco this and political whatever, but real life ... " Luke windmilled the joint. " ... they're in dreamland. You know what I mean?" Suzanne nodded.

Luke lit up and took a deep drag. " ... Dreamland. Oz." he murmured.

"How's Martin these days?" Suzanne, who had been watching him, enquired.

"Oh, he's fine, fine. I mean, in as much as he ever is… fine."

"What does that mean?"

"Oh, you know. He's always kind of ... never really lets himself go. Not, I mean, that he should. I mean ... I value his supply." Suzanne didn't laugh, although Luke meant it as a joke. He changed tack and said soberly: "But he's fine really. You went out with him, didn't you?"

There was a long silence.

Luke coughed uncomfortably. "I guess you don't see him now, then?"

"No. I don't think I've seen him ... for at least a few years."

"Oh, well. You'll have lots to talk about then."

"Lots."

Luke once more found himself at a loss for words, so he looked round the room as though seeing it for the first time. The furniture was comfortable, and surprisingly tasteful considering his father had chosen it. Three deep velvet sofas formed a C around an oak coffee table. There were also a couple of bureaus, elaborate standard lamps, chairs, a dark fireplace. There was other stuff too, which pleased Luke by being uncoordinated. He was not keen on co-ordination.

His eye fell on the bottle of tequila. The level, he noticed, had now reached the J in José.

"Do you smoke this stuff?" he asked solicitously. Suzanne shook her head. Luke sighed. "I'm getting kind of bored with it myself."

"I have something a little stronger. If you like ... "

Luke's face lit up.

Soon he had a crisp piece of foil under his nose with a lighter turning the silver to a purple bruise. The white powder fizzed and Luke took a deep drag before passing it to Suzanne. As the smoke hit his nerves he had the familiar, cosy feeling of a plunger being depressed somewhere round the back of his head, then, as he exhaled, like a syringe slowly sucking all the shit and cobwebs from the space between his ears. It left him with a clear mind and perfect vision. So long as nothing came along to scare him, he'd be feeling good for a while. "Now that hits *the spot*," he told her, shaking his head. "Man, this stuff got so *pure* recently. Amazing. It just keeps getting better and better. It's what you'd have to call a mature industry, right?"

They sat in silence for some minutes, comfortable. Then Luke remembered that he was not alone and decided to make conversation again. "You never used to, actually, did you?" he said.

"What?"

"Take drugs. I was just thinking, you know, that it's kind of strange, considering, that you went out with Martin."

"What's strange?" Suzanne said in a low, hollow voice.

"I know it was a long time ago," Luke backtracked, realizing she was not as stoned as he'd thought. "I just meant ... it's, like, odd that someone like you should go out with someone, ah, like him. Attraction of opposites, I guess." The grandfather clock outside the door ticked loudly. "What exactly do you mean?" Luke was in deep water. "Oh, come on, Suzanne, you were so like ... like ... clean. You know that."

"You can talk. What about you?"

"Uh?"

"Weren't you pretty fucking clean yourself?"

He wished she'd stop.

Suzanne took a deep breath. "I may have been "clean" once." She emphasized the last word as though it had something crude or even humorous about it. "Not any more."

"Well, I can see that ... but it doesn't mean, I mean ... " Luke broke off. The clock really was loud, he noticed uncomfortably.

"Luke, tell me something. What is it that scares you?"

"Pain and death." Luke said promptly.

There was a silence.

Then to his horror she suddenly sniffed phlegmily, and he realized she was crying behind her glasses. She didn't move, except to open her mouth, and then it stopped, and it was as if nothing had happened.

"I am diseased." She whispered hoarsely into the silence.

Luke stared in transfixed confusion into her sunglasses.

## XXII

*Suzanne wasn't sure what she thought of him. But then, she wasn't alone. No one seemed to know — and he was certainly a strange one.*

*Six months had passed since her arrival; in that time she had met dozens, made friends with a few, and she was happy. After the convent, who wouldn't be?*

*Now she knew, at least by sight, almost everyone in the big school dining room. But this one, this Martin, was different. This was the essence of her thought as she watched him discreetly.*

*Carol and Julia were chatting at her side. All of them were enjoying a cup of lukewarm tea. He sat three tables away, in a corner, alone. He had on the heavy greatcoat he always wore and boots marked with mud. These were the standard badges of the rebel. But, Suzanne reflected, he couldn't be a real rebel — he wasn't part of a group. That was the strangest thing. Everyone else was easily defined by the company they kept, their cliques. But he seemed to be alone.*

*He too had a cup of tea. But this time as he raised the mug, his eyes swivelled, meeting hers. After a split second, he smiled. She held his eye, not moving. He raised the mug slightly, a sort of greeting. The corner of her mouth twitched involuntarily. And then she looked away, and then she* was talking about exams to Carol, and when she looked again, he was gone.

Two days later, she was again in the dining room, but this time alone. She had just started eating when he entered. Perhaps she had a premonition, for she lowered her head, and ate steadily. When she next looked up, the greatcoat's muddy hem was only feet away.

"Hi, Suzanne," he said.

She remembered what Julia had said about him, in a tone of disdain: "The chemist's son."

"Hi." She met his eyes at closer range than ever before. Nice, but unexceptional brown eyes. His face too. Nice, but not great. Not beautiful, or handsome, or even very intriguing. But there was something straightforward about him ... and perhaps the fact that he was calm. That was unusual for most of the boys her age.

"Can I sit down?"

"Um, yes." She didn't want to invite him, but she didn't want to be rude. He took the seat at the corner and she smelt something like woodsmoke as he sat. He didn't take his coat off.

"I hear you're an economist," he said quietly.

"What?"

"I heard you're the best in the class. Are you planning to take a degree in it?"

"I really don't know."

There was a long pause. Then he said "Sweet music." Or something that sounded like it. She turned, already frowning. Compliments notwithstanding, she wasn't comfortable with him. These boys with their grubby coats and crumpled packs of cigarettes, tough guys, poseurs ...

"What?" It came out coldly but he didn't flicker.

"In this canteen. Like a hum, like a machine. All these people, two hundred would you say? It's sweet music."

"I never noticed."

"You will. Well, you may. If you listen."

"I can hear. I just don't hear music, exactly." She heard defensive *irritation in her tone, was simultaneously hopeful and fearful that he would go away. He didn't.*

"Music ... It's like ... refraction. And the music is sweet, because we're all still young." He took a deep drink from his mug. Suzanne was all but speechless. She was sure of one thing: no one had ever talked to her this way before. Not knowing what to say, she held her tongue.

He had turned to her. "You're probably thinking that was kind of weird."

"Yes."

"That's OK." Suddenly he was standing. "Come for a smoke?"

"No, I don't."

"OK." He shrugged, apparently unbothered. "Well, I hope I'll see you later." And he was on his way.

Their next encounter came a week later. Again it was in the evening. This time she was with three of her new friends, all of them loudly making their opinions on some boy known. It was after supper, a Saturday. That meant a film, maybe, or more tea. But nothing exciting.

Suddenly he was there, and the girls had fallen quiet. It was the quiet that meant *you* might be cool, but *we* don't know it. He ignored them. "Hi, Suzanne. How do you like stars?"

"What?"

"Come out, and I'll show you something."

"What?"

One of the girls mouthed something, which might have been "creep". But she didn't dare do it out loud, and he ignored her.

"Did you say "stars"?" Again, Suzanne was at a loss, and faintly angered by this fact. If he was trying to make a fool of her ...

"Stars. I thought you would appreciate the beauty. But it's up to you, no pressure."

Why she said yes, she didn't know. But a minute later she was outside in the fresh spring evening air, the tang of that woodsmoke smell beside her.

*"No stars." She observed.*

*"It'll be dark in half an hour. Then you'll see them." He looked down at her. "Suzanne, first, I want to tell you: if you want to turn back, say so, and we will."*

*"Perhaps I should." She laughed nervously. "Where are we going?"*

*"To take a better look at the stars. A vantage point. I think people should look out for the stars."*

*"I don't know what you mean."*

*"You will. Are you afraid?"*

*"No."*

*"Good. Courage will take you a long way."*

*They began to walk in silence. Over the ridge of earth that bordered the school to the east and along a muddy path that led down towards the wooded valley. Her heart was beating somewhat fast. But it was true: she did not feel afraid.*

*After a while she said: "Tell me what you mean, look out for the stars?"*

*"I mean, basically, that we ought to look up and away more often. A long way up and away. For a change."*

*"I don't get it."*

*"Well, people usually look down. At desks. The floor. Books. Themselves. I don't think these things are sufficient. I mean, I think if you want to find the truth, find out what's really worth believing in and what's not you have to go out and search for it." He grinned. " I mean ... it isn't going to pop up in the A-Level syllabus is it? So, I think people should look up, not just down. I think we should ... push back ... "*

*He fell silent, thoughtful, as if he wasn't sure where the thought went next.*

*"You're quite a philosopher."*

*He smiled, but didn't answer.*

*They walked on, towards the woods. They were now out of sight of the school, and it was growing dark. Suzanne was shivering slightly, she thought with the coolness of the evening.*

*But still not afraid.*

"*Come on, where are we going?*"

"*To look at the stars, like I said. Don't be afraid, Suzanne. If you push back your fear, you can do anything.*"

"*I'm not afraid.*"

*Nor was she, though it was the strangest conversation of her life.*

*Once inside the woods, it was much darker, and the little light left was fading fast. She heard him say "Take my hand." And to her surprise, she reached out for him. His palm was soft and warm. He led her into the darkness.*

*For a long time there was no sound but their breathing and the shuffle of their feet on the path. Despite the gathering gloom, he never once faltered. About fifteen minutes later they were still walking and she knew that she was completely lost, dependent upon him. She began to hear strange forest noises on either side, remembered his promise, and wondered. But she trusted him. She had no idea why.*

*Suddenly, they broke out of the shadows onto a bank. A glittering slice of silver split the forest, swirling softly. In the centre of the small clearing they had come to was a great oak. She realized suddenly that they had come to the place where the bad boys were reputed to go — the Rope. The Rope was indeed a rope: a long cord attached to a branch of the oak, overhanging the river.*

"*Let me ask you something,*" *he said, halting and turning to her. There was a long pause.* "*If you could ... if you could, go out, actually reach the stars — other galaxies, planets, travel there ... not knowing what you'd find, maybe heaven maybe hell ... would you?*"

*Without having to think, she nodded. And she was strangely elated by his smile.*

## XXIII

Maria had found a tablecloth somewhere and also a Royal Doulton dinner set. Six places were laid in the dining room next to the kitchen. There were napkins in beaten copper holders, the lace tablecloth, candles in candelabra and Baccarat crystal. When Luke came in and saw Chloe and Eliot and Maria fussing round with bottles and sideplates he was stunned. Everything was perfect ... resurrected.

Maria looked up. "I'm afraid it doesn't look like your friend Martin is going to make it," she said.

"Yeah. Where is His Royal Highness anyway?" Eliot demanded casually. "Or should I say, where's his drugs?"

"Eliot, come on;" Maria ordered. "Pour the wine." Eliot seemed amused, but he started to do as he was told.

"Has anyone seen Suzanne?" Maria went on. "Eliot, maybe you could look for her, I'll do the wine ... "

"Orders, orders ... " Eliot chuckled. As he left he whispered to Luke: "Fuck. She's a fine woman, Luke, I'm telling you."

Luke looked at him and said tonelessly: "I used to cook, do you remember?"

Eliot frowned. "Yeah. You were pretty good too — weren't you? I should try it again if I were you." He went out noisily.

"Why not?" Luke said to himself. "Why?" Another voice answered plaintively.

Suzanne was half floating, half back-paddling through the greenish water of the indoor pool. Eliot entered the glass-walled room and looked round expectantly. Having followed a provocative trail of clothing along the passage thus far, he wasn't sure what to expect. He wasn't disappointed. She was wearing a pair of shorts of some kind, but her breasts were bare to the world, breaking the surface as brown and perfect as he'd always imagined.

She turned and looked at him.

Eliot put his hands on his hips and leered back with unconcealed delight.

"You're staring at me. What, do I turn you on?" She said quietly but distinctly. Eliot grinned his answer.

Then she said something less clear. It sounded like "I'd really like it if you'd masturbate."

Eliot wasn't quite sure he'd caught it. "What did you say?"

"If I'm turning you on. It'd turn me on. If you'd masturbate. Here. Now. I might even ... " She grinned and pushed herself underwater.

Eliot was thunderstruck. But not quite overwhelmed. The weekend was going so well, so far, that just about anything seemed possible. This was *something* but he was on a roll ... who knew. Maybe it was a test, even? After all, not many blokes would be buzz enough to ... Eliot glanced around to see that it was quiet. It was. He felt his excitement grow. All right then! Double or quits, if she wanted to play tough. Without a word Eliot undid his fly, loosened his penis and took a firm hold on it. The truth was, it didn't take much. The sight of her there had been enough, her words like oil on a fire. As blood pumped in, Suzanne pushed out for the ladder and began to climb out. Her loose shorts hung around her hips, every curve outlined. He began to breathe more heavily, his hand moving rhythmically up and down. Her nipples stood erect, hard ... to touch those nipples, was suddenly all that Eliot wanted in this world. She came round the edge of the swimming pool, walking slowly and sexily, her gypsy-dark lips slightly parted. What a promise was there! She came right up to him. His member strained and heaved for those breasts. She stood there, as he masturbated in front of her. "Eliot," she said, "you're one in a million. I almost like you."

"Yeah?" Eliot grinned some more. "No almost about it on this side, baby."

She smiled. "Let it go." Eliot hesitated, then dropped his cock. It stood firm, waiting urgently. She edged closer. "Close your eyes." He hesitated. "Go on," she said. "If you want something." He obeyed. Her hand closed round his baton of muscle, he took a sharp breath and shivered. Her voice was like aural pornography, inches from his ear. "Imagine, Eliot, if my legs were up in the air, if I was crying out for you, desperate for your cock up inside me, "Fuck me, do it to me, pump me, hard, hard, *fuck* me!" would you like that?"

Her hand slid down into his trousers and gently took his testicles. "Ah, Jesus ... " Eliot gasped.

She leaned forward suddenly tightening her grip. "Or, Eliot," she whispered hoarsely, imagine if I was to twist these and drag you round the swimming pool till they came off in my hand. Imagine if I was to get a knife and slice your prick up like salami and throw it to the fish in the river ... "

Eliot's eyes popped open. She wasn't smiling. "If you're going to dream, Eliot, watch out for nightmares." She squeezed just hard enough to make him whimper, then let go and walked away.

Eliot stared down at his suddenly limp adjunct of flesh, dumbfounded.

Eliot returned to the kitchen alone and announced that Suzanne would join them later. He seemed subdued. Maria shrugged and brought four plates from the kitchen. "Baked squid with rillettes d'olive," she said, setting them down. On each one the squid swam in a dark, fragrant sauce.

"Pretty good." Chloe allowed grudgingly. Luke nodded and Maria smiled. Eliot didn't seem to notice much and began to eat automatically.

The others noticed his strange mood and also fell to silent eating. Finally, Eliot looked up, shook his head as though clearing it of something alien, and gave a sudden, determined grunt. "Maria, this is the business!" he said, and raised his glass almost violently. "*Shit*, we're having a good time!" He shook his head and suddenly slumped back in his seat. "Jesus, look at us!" He peered round the table. The others waited reluctantly. "Look at us! Old friends! Why the hell don't we do this more often?"

Chloe snorted.

Eliot ignored her. "It's so good to get away from the city, you know? A bit of grass, scenery, and like, most important, old friends ... "

"You old romantic." Chloe sneered.

"No, it's true." He emptied his glass. "This is a fine weekend. A great weekend. I really mean it. What more could anyone want than a loyal, wonderful best friend ... " He raised his glass to Luke, who looked surprised, " ... My beautiful cousin Maria here ... "

Chloe sighed. "Eliot, if you're going to take acid, you might do it elsewhere."

Eliot laughed benignly. " ... And our good, sweet-natured friend Chloe. That's a dry humour you've got, babe."

"And a mighty sentimental vein *you've* got."

Eliot shook his head and said: "Chloe, I just want us all to have a nice time ... I really do."

"Oh, go fuck yourself. Christ, Eliot, haven't you got any... any decency?"

Eliot was taken aback. "What?"

"What are you, forgetting something?"

"I'n not with you."

"Your fucking miserable personality for one thing." her anger surprised everyone, even Eliot. He felt his sudden meekness and brotherly love begin to dissolve. "What the hell ... "

"You want me to spell it out?"

"Look Chloe, you haven't even seen me for five years, what's your fucking problem?" In fact, he was already beginning to guess.

"Just shut-up, Eliot. I know what you're like and you haven't changed."

Eliot looked bemused. "Honey, if we're talking about changes, have you? Still see yourself as little Miss Romantic? Sheeet."

"I went for a romantic walk this afternoon, Eliot," Chloe snarled. "Along the river. Right round the school. I was thinking of Charlie. Remember him?"

Eliot was ready by now. "Yeah, I remember him. And?"

"Well then, shut up."

"Who was Charlie?" Maria asked. Eliot answered quickly: "Just a friend. There was an accident. Unfortunately. And," he met Chloe's stare, "I don't see what it's got to do with anything."

"All right," Luke said tensely, "let's change the subject."

"Glad to." Eliot muttered, and turned to Maria. "Maria," he said, "you're hot. This shit you've cooked is excellent."

"Thank you."

"You should be a chef. What subjects do you want to do?"

"Sorry?"

"At school, school."

"Oh, I don't know."

"Hah! Bad attitude. As Doc Wolff would say. He was our old headmaster. Left under mysterious circumstances. And then the school closed down. Talking of which ... " he turned to Chloe, obviously looking for a truce, " ... I don't suppose you ever found anything out about that — you know, living with Suzanne?"

Chloe looked at him ironically. "Now, whatever made you think that?"

"No reason. Anyway, I'm only interested. No need to bite my head off." But Chloe had stopped listening. Behind Eliot, Martin had appeared in the doorway.

## XXIV

"The Rope," he said.

"The Rope." Suzanne agreed, shivering slightly though it was hardly cold.

"I'll show you." Martin went to the tree and shinned up with agility. Suzanne sat down on a dry log nearby and watched. Martin climbed along the long branch which reached over the river and swung easily onto the rope, which he then slid down. Suzanne saw that there was a knot tied near the bottom of it and that a baton of some kind was tied in the knot, as an elephant would carry a stick in its trunk. Martin put his boots on this and began to work up a swinging motion. After a minute, his swing took him up over the bank and he jumped. As the rope swung back on its return flight, he caught it and fastened it under a heavy stone left for this purpose on the bank.

"Nice work, Tarzan." Suzanne said. Martin grinned, his teeth shining in the light. "Want a go?" he challenged.

"I don't mind."

"Take your jacket off then. Otherwise it'll get in your way." Suzanne obeyed, and left it neatly folded on the log. She felt a little exposed suddenly and crossed her arms. Martin took the rope out from under the stone. He showed her how to hang on high up before jumping off so that she wouldn't end up knee deep in the river. Then he handed her the thick knobbly rope.

Taking it, she felt her heart begin to throb, but she was not afraid. "I'm going to take my shoes off." she announced, and handed the heavy cord back for a moment. Their hands brushed, she pulled away self-consciously.

She took it off him again, and as she stepped back to prepare for the take-off run, the knot creaked in the branches overhead. She felt an urge to make some comment like: "I suppose this is where I find you loosened it up there." But checked herself.

Then she ran, barefoot over the compressed dark earth, and with a final exertion flew off the bank, the bottom of the rope thwacking off under and behind her. She gave an involuntary whoop as Martin applauded from the bank.

"Now," he called, "you'll have to hang on tight."

"What?"

"I'm going to join you."

"What? *How can you?*"

"Just hold on tight."

"But Martin, you can't ... " Martin wasn't listening. He backed off a few paces from the bank, waited until the rope was in mid-swing towards him then ran forward, jumped, and caught it a foot above Suzanne's head. She gasped with delicious panic as the rope jerked, then again with relief when neither of them fell off. Martin lowered himself. "Take your feet off the baton for a second, then you can put them on mine." Suzanne did as she was told. She was holding the rope with both hands in front of her breasts. He, when he had his feet secure, held on with one hand above her head and gave her a wide grin.

"Oh, God!" she exclaimed, half delighted, half terrified.

"Were you frightened?" he asked.

"Of course not!" Suzanne scoffed. "You think *you* can frighten *me*?"

"I doubt it. You seem pretty intrepid." Suzanne felt pleased and bit her lip. She realized suddenly that he was talking to her again. "Do you know what this is?" he was asking. In his free hand he was holding a tiny locket. As the swing of the rope became less formidable, he flicked it open. Inside was a white powder. Suzanne tensed and looked up at him. "No." She whispered.

"No?" He repeated. "Here, can you hold it?" Suzanne freed one of her hands and did as she was asked. Martin wet a finger with his tongue, dipped it into the powder, then rubbed it back into his mouth around the gums of his teeth. Suzanne watched him doubtfully. When he had finished he looked at her. "Trust me," he said quietly. Then he repeated the operation, but pressed his finger to her mouth. Closing her eyes, hardly believing what was happening, she felt his soft, cold finger move gently past her lips, and almost immediately there was a sensation in her gums like champagne bubbles popping; Martin took the locket off her, and she heard a click as it closed. But she did not open her eyes. There was a warm undercurrent of breath on her cheek, the smell of him, that woodsmoke smell, then his lips, pressed gently as anything to hers. "I must be drunk," she thought. Then she sighed and opened her mouth; moments later, her tongue exploded with an extraordinary lightness. The roof of her mouth seemed to drift gently away, leaving the very essence of her being in her tongue and teeth. "Stars ... " she murmured.

## XXV

Maria saw a man in his 'twenties with short dark hair and tired but careful eyes. He was leaning against the door jamb, hands deep in the pockets of his coat. Beneath the coat he wore a crumpled white shirt without a tie.

"Sorry," he said. "I came in the back way."

No one moved.

He pushed himself free of the jamb and came forward. "Chloe. Eliot." He nodded at them. "What's going on? I wasn't expecting a party."

"Well," Luke said uncertainly. "Really, we had a change of plan and decided to come down and join you. Is that, er, OK?"

The newcomer shrugged. "Especially if someone's cooking."

"We laid a place for you." Maria said, standing. "But we weren't sure when you'd get here. Will you sit down?"

Martin slipped out of his coat. "I hope I haven't forgotten you?" He said to Maria, looking at her closely. "You weren't at Elysia?"

"No," Maria said. "I came with Eliot. Would you like to catch up or join us where we are?"

"Anywhere." Martin took a seat opposite Luke and Chloe, next to Eliot. He gestured at the remaining place set.

"What's this? Are people arriving in shifts?"

"In shifts." Suzanne said behind him. She came into the room wearing a navy blue cotton dress with a wide leather belt inlaid with silver. Her hair was still damp.

Maria, hovering above her chair saw Martin freeze. "Thought I'd give you a surprise, Martin," she said, apparently casually. Martin turned and watched her move slowly through the shadowy room. "You succeeded," he murmured.

Maria cleared her throat through the tension. "Eliot," she said uncertainly, "are you still eating, or can I take your plate?"

* * *

Luke went round the table filling fresh glasses with his father's best Mersault.

"Did you come by car?" Maria enquired.

"Yes. Yes I did."

"It's just, no one heard you arrive."

"I parked a little way up the lane. I went to the stable to get the key, and then I realized the lights were on. So I came straight in."

"Crept in, I would say." Suzanne commented. "I saw you." Martin returned her stare for a second, then looked away.

"You could have been thieves."

"Of course."

Eliot brought the dorade to the table in a deep steaming casserole. "Perhaps one of you could serve, while I get the vegetables ... " Maria called over her shoulder. Martin was nearest, but Eliot leaned over abruptly and said "I'll do it."

Martin retracted his hand, raised his glass equably and said: "Well, you people are really living it up." And smiled pleasantly across the table at Suzanne.

* * *

The meal resumed with small talk, which Martin seemed to initiate and encourage whilst managing to spend most of his time eating hungrily. Then a sort of calm descended. The clink of glasses, the tapping of cutlery and the fine dinner and wine silenced them all. The lack of conversation seemed quite natural. When Martin had finished he turned to Maria.

"Thank you. You saved my life," he said. Maria smiled uncertainly.

"So," he continued, "how did you all happen to get together?" He looked at Suzanne.

"I live with Chloe." Suzanne said. "And she met Luke and Eliot last night."

"I see."

"And Maria," Suzanne added, "is with Eliot."

"Lucky man. This is excellent cooking."

"Eliot's my cousin. We're not together." Maria said quietly. Eliot looked up in transparent surprise. Maria sighed. "Well, if you've all had enough, I'll get the dessert ... " There were murmurs of assent. She began to gather up the plates in silence and Eliot said sharply: "I'll help you."

Once the two of them had gone to the kitchen, Luke pulled out some cigarettes and offered them round. Everyone except Suzanne accepted.

"So, what's going on, Martin?" Luke asked, leaning back. "How's tricks?"

"Fine; fine, thanks." Martin nodded, lighting the cigarette.

"They say you're in 'commodities'." Chloe said. "Doing well?"

"So-so. You take it seriously ... and have a little luck. Things work out." He looked at Suzanne, inhaling heavily. "And how's life treating *you* these days?"

"I do a little modelling. Ends meet."

"I often thought we should have stayed in touch."

"I don't think that would have been a good idea."

At that moment Eliot and Maria returned from the kitchen where they, and Eliot in particular, had been talking in lowered voices. Maria looked cool and collected, but Eliot was noticeably red. He banged down the dishes he was carrying and sank as though drained into his seat.

"Pear and marron glacé Dome," Maria announced, placing a pastry dish in the centre of the table. "I hope you like it."

"Looks fantastic," Luke said.

"What is it?" Chloe demanded suspiciously.

"It's pear ice-cream with crystallized chestnuts on a base of ice. Please, serve yourselves."

"I seem to have come to the right place," Martin said.

After dessert everyone went into the sitting room. Despite the wind rising outside, it was quite warm. Luke, licking his lips thirstily went straight to the drinks cabinet asking what everyone was having. Martin and Eliot both opted for single malt, Suzanne and Maria stuck to the wine they'd started at supper. Chloe asked for a vodka tonic. For himself, Luke constructed a very large American Iced Tea and drank half of it in one gulp.

"Cheers," Martin said.

Maria suddenly laughed, and everyone turned to look at her. "I thought one of you was going to say: "To old times," she said. "Aren't you?"

Suzanne swallowed, Luke peered into his drink and Eliot and Chloe both looked suddenly uncomfortable. But Martin said: "Good idea. After all, they weren't that bad." He looked at Suzanne and raised his glass. "Old times."

Suzanne did not drink, but said: "Do we have to be so pompous? Can't we have some music, Luke?" Eliot coughed and mumbled: "Good thinking."

"Just spare us the Clash, please." Chloe said drily. and everyone began to shuffle around more easily.

While Eliot and Chloe chose a record, Martin came up beside Luke and said, "Can I have a quick word?"

"What is it?"

"I was wondering how long you're likely to be staying down here."

"Oh, the weekend. I don't think anyone has to get back ... why?"

"I may have to stay out of London for a few more days. If I could stay here it'd really help me."

"Of course you can. Any time."
Martin squeezed Luke's shoulder. "Thanks, Luke. Really."

"No problem." After hesitating for a second, he added, "Um, by the way, you didn't happen to bring anything along, you know ... I think we're down to our last line here ... "

"I nearly forgot." Martin pulled a folded brown envelope from his pocket and handed it over. "Here you go."

"Ah, that's great, Mart, thanks. Hey, how much is it? I'll give you some cash." Martin waved a hand. "Forget it." But Luke looked up from opening the envelope with surprise. "Hey, this is a lot ... "

"It's yours."

Luke protested weakly, but Martin had already shifted away towards Suzanne. She was sitting on a sofa a little way apart from the others. "Hi," he said.

"No, Martin." Her voice sounded tired.

"No what?"

"Don't bother." He sat down at the end of the sofa and shut his eyes, touching the lids with his fingers. Then he said: "Well at least tell me, which one of these people are you with?" Suzanne's lips tightened, but then he was looking at her again. "None of them."

"You came alone."

"No, I didn't come alone. I came with my friends."

"You came with your friends, OK. And you knew I'd be here." He waited, but she was silent. "You act like I'm the last person on earth you want to see but you're here."

"I didn't know you'd be here until we set off."

"But you didn't get out of the car, apparently."

Seeing that he was only angering her, he changed tack. He leaned forward and tried to be sweetly reasonable: "Look ... " She rolled her eyes. "Look, I was just going to say, that I'm going to need help soon.

100

Tomorrow. I'm in trouble, and I need a favour."

"No."

"Please."

"Good God! Why ask me of all people? And what *are* you doing down here, Martin?"

"I'm looking for help, that's it."

She stood up quickly, almost bumping into Luke who was approaching with a mirror. " ... Have a line?" he asked cheerily. Suzanne took it and sat down abruptly. She took the rolled up banknote and with a quick movement snorted a white line off the face. Martin watched. He felt a tingling of distaste, but was relieved at the pathetic-triumphant look she gave him when she looked up. Perhaps she just wanted to prove her point. "Well, I heard about this," he murmured, nodding at the mirror, "but I never believed it till now." Suzanne stared at him, and he thought for a second she would spit in his face.

* * *

Luke, bouncing on the balls of his feet, his glass refilled, a sunny morning finally dawning in his head, went over to Chloe and sat on the arm of her chair. Chloe appeared not to notice him and went on talking to Maria.

" ... I was kicked out of classes for the last six weeks, all I did was read a couple of copies of the 'Economist', you know, the morning of the exam, and I got through on that ... O-levels, A-Levels, GCSE, whatever you call it now, it's just a game."

"I don't know ... " Luke interrupted. "I didn't do any work for A-Levels and I didn't get any either."

"Yeah, well ... *maybe*, Luke, you're not exactly a representative intellect if you know what I mean ... " Luke knew he was significantly stoned because he didn't even feel hurt.

Eliot took the mirror when it was passed to him and moodily snorted up a thick line. The cause of his umbrage was the girl with the extraordinarily blue and inscrutable eyes on the chair nearby, listening to Luke and Chloe. She had just made it quite clear, though without rancour or even emotion, that she would not be sleeping with him that night. "Don't take it personally, Eliot. I can't even see where I'm going myself at the moment. But something needs me to keep moving." What the *fuck* was that supposed to mean? In barely a day he had won and lost the sexiest chick he'd seen in months, and had Suzanne dump all over him. Chloe was needlessly bringing that old business with Charlie up as if to taunt him ... for *what*? And the real mystery was, as far as he could see, *he hadn't put a foot wrong.*

\* \* \*

Outside, drops of rain fell fitfully in the hot wind. In the far distance, a thunderstorm was audible between songs.

Luke poured his seventh shot of strong alcohol, in this case vodka, re-lit the cigarette in his mouth just in case it had gone out, and stumbled back to the armchair he was beginning to feel was home. Martin was in the chair next to him, apparently asleep. By the French windows, Eliot was dancing, after a fashion, to 'Radio Clash'. His glass of tequila became an outsize plectrum while his free hands clutched at an invisible line of frets as four Bose Electrostats pumped the music round the room and out into the Dorset night. Chloe watched from the sofa with an expression of incredulous contempt. Suzanne stood a few yards beyond the windows, outside, staring at the stars.

Luke watched them all. He loved them all, every one, like the tenderest lover, for a slow, alcohol-induced moment. He thought he could love them forever if they would only freeze, just as they were, and never move again.

## XXVI

Eliot went out to relieve himself, and bumped into Chloe entering her room. "Hey baby," he grunted without much hope. "Are you lonely this Christmas?"

"Fuck off, Eliot." It wasn't even said angrily. Just like he was some fly. And then she shut the door on him. Eliot was flabbergasted.

In another part of the house, Suzanne waylaid Luke in a corridor. "Listen, Luke," she said swiftly. "I'd appreciate it if you'd stay with me tonight."

"Oh ... not altogether easy ... "

"I don't want anything, except that you stay in my room."

"Why?"

"Just do it for me, would you?"

"Well, OK…"

"Thanks. I'll be back in a minute." She bundled Luke through the door to her bedroom then continued down the corridor to the room which Martin had taken. She entered without knocking. He was sitting on the bed, his shirt off, examining some kind of a camera.

"I just thought I'd tell you, in case you get romantic in the middle of the night ... I'm with Luke."

"Luke?"

"Yeah. So stay away." She slammed the door and went back to her room. There she stripped off her clothes before Luke's amazed eyes, threw herself down on the bed and closed her eyes.

## XXVII

*When Martin had brought them both safely back to the bank, helped her into his overcoat as it was growing cold, and they had started the long walk back, she said: "I think I know what that stuff was ... the stuff you gave me." Martin laughed and put his arm round her shoulders. She responded a little uncertainly by putting her hand, peeping out of the arm of the big coat, round his waist. "No, really," she said.*

"Well?" Martin asked.

"My brother Alex — you probably remember him, he was here ... he's involved in that too."

"Alex Baez was your brother?"

"You remember him?"

"Sure I do. But not well. He was one of the Black Dragon generation, wasn't he?"

"Yes, he was here then."

"They were pretty cool"

"You may think so. I don't."

He laughed. "You sound kind of disapproving."

"I am. He actually ... he imports it. That stuff you gave me."

"So he's a businessman. "

She gave him a challenging look. "Perhaps. But when my father found out, it gave him a heart attack. He nearly died. Not many businesses do that."

"I'm sorry." She didn't know if he was apologizing or referring to her father. But she relaxed.

Martin was silent. He seemed to be thinking, when she glanced at his face. She was glad that he was taking her seriously. She said: "I hope you're not like my brother. Not in that respect, at least. She smiled up at him. "You remind me of Alex. And I love him, I really do." She frowned. "He's strong, and that's good. But what he does with his strength is bad. I do believe in good and bad."

"Yeah? Who's winning?"

She pretended to hit him. "You're laughing!"

"No. I swear."

She sighed. "You're probably thinking this is something to do with the fact that I went to a convent before Elysia. Well, it is, but not in that way. It was when I was there, and the nuns were constantly going on about good and evil all the time, and anyone could see that it was completely irrelevant to our lives ... I mean, no one paid the slightest attention. So I started thinking about it for myself. And I realized, it's very simple: good is about doing things for others' sake, bad is about doing them for your own sake, only. So — the thing about Alex is, that he's not working for other people. He's working for himself. OK, so you'll say so are most people. But not to the same degree. Selling drugs is further down the scale of selfish actions, therefore worse, than most things." She paused, waiting for his response.

"And you called me a philosopher?"

She smiled at his smile. "It's just reality. But you're still laughing."

"I'm not laughing." Martin considered for a while. "Did Alex?"

"What?"

"Laugh."

She blushed. "Alex doesn't listen to schoolgirls. He once said no sane person over the age of eighteen believes in good and bad. But he's wrong.

And of course, he has a vested interest in being cynical anyway." She looked for his reaction.

"So let me get this straight. Selling drugs is OK, so long as it's for selfless reasons."

"It might be if it were. But I'm not sure it ever is."

In other words ... " Martin laughed, " ... you're going to give me hell on this one."

"Well ... "

"Listen ... " but he hesitated. She nodded to encourage him. "OK. You've been frank with me, Suzanne, and I appreciate it. So let me be frank with you. I hate sounding corny, so I'm only going to say it once, all right?" Surprised, she nodded again. "I don't know about good and bad, but whether we're talking about drugs or anything else it's not my intention to hurt anyone. All I want, Suzanne, is to find a way of life that's true to me, myself. What I don't want, I don't want to end up believing I'm doing well because I've got two kids, a car and four bedrooms in Bromley like my parents. I know there's more than that out there, there's got to be. I want my independence, and I want the stars, Suzanne, and I'm going to keep reaching for them until I get what I want. And like it or not, you're the same. I knew it the moment I saw you. You came out with me this evening, took a risk. We're both searching for something out of the ordinary ... and we could both search together."

His words produced a warm glow in her veins. She was, she observed with a detached, wry disbelief, attracted to him. To his independence, his maturity in comparison with the other boys his age. If only she could harness that strength and make it positive, before it got too late — as it probably had with Alex. And why shouldn't she be the one to reach out and help him? She glanced up. Not handsome, but strong. But what was he *thinking*? Well, now was the time to find out.

"Martin ... " she hesitated, "I can't read your mind. And I don't know much about boys. I don't know whether you thought ... whether you took me out this evening because you," she blushed and looked down, "you were thinking about going out with me or something ... " Determinedly she *forced herself to meet his eyes again.* "But I want you to know, that whatever you think — and I'm sorry if I've interpreted it all wrong — if I ever did go out with you then I'd want you to give up things like drugs. OK?"

His voice was soft, and it was too dark to see his face. "Is that a proposal?"

It was so hard to say these things. "Don't play with me," she said hesitantly. "I don't know why ... I don't know, I mean, why me?"

It was so dark now, the voice was almost disembodied. "It's actually quite simple." It said quietly. "I need you, Suzanne."

## XXVIII

Martin caught a couple of hours sleep in a chair in his room, but didn't undress. Before dawn he went quietly downstairs, drank a glass of water in the kitchen and left the house for his car.

His first destination was the home of Nadeine's friend, Marie Louise Perroux, in the county of Wiltshire. He drove along deserted country lanes, passing now and again through silent, empty villages which in darkness wore a strange and sinister air. After a while the sun began to rise across the hills to his right, magnificent and solemn. Martin hardly noticed.

After an hour or so he came to a spot near the address Nadeine had given him. He parked the car in a secluded lay-by, got out and opened the boot. Inside was a jumble of equipment purchased from a photographic shop in Salisbury the previous afternoon. Prominent was a modern, lightweight video camcorder; he left it and took out a small Polaroid with a zoom and a pair of high-powered binoculars. Finally he locked the boot and set off across the fields on a long cross-country walk.

\* \* \*

He returned a few hours later, replaced the things he was carrying (which included several exposures of a transit van in a lay-by and a man with binoculars apparently bird watching near the main road) and drove away east. He kept, as he had on the first leg of his journey, to secondary roads. As he passed through a new set of ancient hamlets, it occurred to him that they had lost the faintly hostile air he had remarked earlier and, in the bright morning light, returned schizophrenically to sleepy quaintness. It all mattered little to Martin, however. He was thinking of Sussex, of the place he was headed for now, and of the three or four hours he would have to spend there marking out the territory. And all the time, in the back of his mind lay the most important question. He was wondering if his nerve would hold.

# XXIX

Eliot awoke to find himself alone in the sitting room. He was still wearing his trousers, but his shirt and vest had disappeared. Record covers, glasses and ashtrays littered the floor. A shaft of sunlight illuminated the corner where he, and the leather armchair he was collapsed in, were.

Having forced his apparently glued-together eyelids apart, he ran an experimental tongue along the roof of his mouth. It moved as though across the surface of a rock. He made no further movement.

At times like this, when Eliot found himself with a *real* hangover, there were a number of options. First, to reach for the bottle again and head for unconsciousness. But like everything else these days, that didn't seem to work as well as it once had. It merely deferred payment, nowadays. Second was to clog up with pills and try to sleep it off. Eliot wasn't sure he had the stomach, or indeed the pills, for that either. Third was to declare war and go and do something drastically energetic, taking the enemy by surprise.

And the only real option was the third one, do or die.

Speculating on this, Eliot considered for a moment running upstairs and raping Maria in her bedroom. The thought reminded him of her inexplicable, perfectly polite but somehow utterly damning refusal to sleep with him. "Bitch." He thought and wanted her to want him. The fantasy drifted away.

He could make breakfast, he supposed, but the thought of frying food and the smells put him off. He wasn't hungry anyway.

The thing to do, he suddenly realized, was to get out. The sun was shining — he twisted in his seat and felt his head complain — yes, the sun was shining. He would take an early Sunday morning walk. Perhaps along the river.

He eased himself upright, grimacing at the weight of his limbs. Dimly, he looked around for his shirt.

Ten minutes later he was on the riverpath. The country, green and bright under an infinitely wide and spacious blue sky was silent and peaceful. The decisive movement had already made him feel better, and he walked with a confident step.

Eliot did not really consider himself a country person. Basically he preferred the noise and bustle of the city and felt more or less at home in the anonymity. He was however much attached to the idea of country weekends.

Luxury meant a great deal to him. Apart from the times when he was able to live off Luke's benison he had few pleasures. This was essentially because, deep down, Eliot considered himself a very superior being, much superior to the task of ordinary work; and furthermore, as an optimist, part of him believed that he had little more to do than wait for his innate eminence to become apparent.

The problem was, the world's tardiness in recognizing his abilities. As he approached the end of his first quarter century on the planet, he couldn't help wondering whether his file might have been mislaid.

From the Millhouse, the riverpath led first through a swampy, thick and brushy area and then entered the outskirts of the ancient woods known in school days as the Garden of Eden.

Eliot had many recollections of the Garden. His basic confidence, amongst adolescents often crippled by insecurity and paranoia, plus his occasional role in the school's 1st XV rugby team (he was a substitute), had given him a position of some small esteem and consequent success. Success capped, as he did not fail to remember, by his eight-month affair with the beautiful Moira. His feelings today diverged sharply on this recollection. On the one hand, it was proof — were it needed — that he was indeed special; the most beautiful girl in the school had chosen *him*. On the other hand, there was the mysterious issue of why it had all come to an end so suddenly, why she had so abruptly stopped seeing him and showed so little sign (to his immense surprise) of missing him thereafter. He remembered his last day with her well, had frequently dwelt on it trying to work out what he'd done wrong. They'd been in Paris with his old roommate Ross, his mother had had the immeasurably bad taste to have a stroke, and he'd had to make a sudden departure. And she'd never spoken to him again. It had niggled ever since.

Perhaps it all explained by the simple fact that she was a nutcase. The last Eliot had heard, she'd dropped out of Oxford a couple of years ago with a nervous breakdown, and spent most of her time in a clinic ever since.

The river widened somewhat, and began to veer away to the south. The woods on the other bank gave way to another long, flat field, where later in the day fishermen would sit patiently with their rods at fifty yard intervals.

It wasn't quite as he remembered it, but he couldn't help noticing how his memory was faintly stirred and how things and faces he had completely forgotten were beginning to come back. This he found annoying, since in his heart he regarded Elysia as one more place that had failed to recognize his potential and therefore hardly worthy of recollection. But as his hangover receded, the memories came back, sometimes surprising him with their clarity.

On impulse he turned off the river path, up the bank and across a narrow lane into what had been known as Despond Valley. It was a very thick wooded area on a direct cross-route to the school. Here most of the dens had been built. There in the Gazebo he had first touched that strawberry blonde — whose name he couldn't remember. Here in Freddie's Hole, that drunken evening, it was — another one whose name he couldn't quite recall. He found himself smiling.

He passed after a while a spot on which Martin had stopped him once, a summer's evening ... The leaving party night in fact, the night before they'd all left. A place called the Black Dragon, where there had been all that trouble years ago. Dodgy place, spooky. What had Martin said? "What are you going to do? Now it's over." Exactly that. He'd been having a piss, and Martin had appeared out of nowhere like a ghost. His talking to him at all had surprised Eliot more than the question itself, strange though it was. They had never had much in common, and until his surprising get-together with the lovely Suzanne, Eliot had had him down as a bit of a weirdo.

"I'm going home." Eliot had replied, nonplussed, anxious to make his way back underground where some red-head and much cheap plonk waited. "Home." Martin had echoed, and then with a ghost of a smile, "*Going* home? Going *home? Don't you know that's a non-sequitur, Eliot?"* Then he had stared at him for a second, and then just disappeared into the undergrowth again.

That was strange. But Martin was unpredictable. Eliot didn't understand Martin, which didn't trouble him, and didn't understand why he was now well off while Eliot himself was not, which did. There had been a lot of strange rumours about Martin at school — of course, he'd ended up the number one pusher, but that wasn't what was meant. It was said that he'd done some really bad things. But then, he was the sort of person about whom rumours would spread. Bit of a loner, the worst type of loner. Certainly never deserved someone like Suzanne.

He turned away, and realized that if he mounted the incline on his left, he would find himself overlooking the school. But it was a long haul, and he wasn't sure if he had the energy.

"What are you going to do? Now it's over." Pretty odd. But then people tended to say weird things to each other at that age. Eliot had never really seen the attraction of it, himself ...

" ... Going home ... " Suddenly, he decided to climb the incline.

Although there was a bed of bracken and general forest floor, the going was muddy and the ascent more difficult than he'd expected. After barely ten yards, he found himself puffing painfully. He'd all but managed to forget his hangover until now, and it hit back with a vengeance. But for some reason, he did not give up. Gripping on to the hanging parts of the trees, or to creepers and roots on the ground, he pulled himself forward. His shoes and feet first became heavy with mud, then soggily wet. Sweat broke out, itching as it awoke salt rivers from the previous night's activity. As he lunged for branches to hang on to, the shaken foliage sent showers of water pouring over him. Thickets of gorse tore at his arms and clothes.

Halfway there, he stopped and cursed, stretching his aching back and limbs. He felt dizzy. But after a moment he continued upwards, urgent in his movements.

Eventually he crawled to the last hurdle, a rusty barbed wire fence, somehow scaled it without shredding himself too much, and stumbled up to the brow of the hill a few feet away. There he collapsed, disregarding the damp grass beneath him.

After a few minutes, when his breath came easier, he turned onto his back and hoisted himself up on to his elbows.

Before and below him lay the excessively vast Victorian C of the main building surrounded by a haphazard jumble of more recent extensions, lawns and playing fields. In the tower, the glass clock-face shone in the early sun like a giant crystal. The Japanese company that had bought the place had landscaped the gardens and sandblasted the walls clean.

"Shitty place." He thought mildly, and wondered why he'd put so much effort into getting up there. What was there to see? The roof under which he'd spent five largely unspectacular years? Still panting a little, he looked round. Countryside, green, lush and ancient, stretched as far as the eye could see, the horizon broken only by the odd cottage. Somehow the whole space had an air of affluence, of ease. It made him uneasy. Five years spent here, under these auspices. If he thought about it, he could remember the interior, most of the grounds that surrounded it, the pubs in the villages and towns around ... In a way, he reflected matter-of-factly, it was the closest he'd ever had to a permanent home. He was an army child, and his Brigadier father had traipsed round the country from one identical base to another like a nomad. He hadn't even seen his parents for a year. Not that he particularly cared. His thoughts turned to Maria.

"Bitch." He thought suddenly. "I could have shown her things ... " He suddenly felt a deep wave of self-pity break over him as he recalled her look. Sympathetic? No. *Pitying*.

Truth was she had thrown him over. A girl of her age throwing him, Eliot, over. Things were really coming to something.

He scanned the horizon. Five years, he thought again. "What are you going to do? Now it's over." "*Going* home? Going *Home*?" A sudden emotion seized him, a sort of desperation that was almost panic. It made him feel cold, rather sick. He closed his eyes but it didn't go away. In a sudden fury he ordered himself to pull himself together — his eyes popped open and he felt better.

The thought had stirred him. It was time to start taking matters in hand. He was Eliot Bennett, a person not to be taken lightly. These chicks — it was time to teach them a lesson. And with a sudden, furious conviction, it occurred to him where to start. He got up and started walking determinedly back down the hill.

## XXX

*During late winter or early spring there were frequent mornings when the sun would rise on a swirling sea of semi-transparent mist. This perfect white and shining vapour, silent and shimmering under the sun on the sparsely populated hills must once have seemed a thing of almost primitive augury: incongruous in the bright light, it was as if it might possess a life of its own, independent and set aside from the normal laws of climate and geography. Few remarked upon it, but many of Elysia's juniors felt an inexplicable unease as they walked bleary-eyed to breakfast, touched by its cold invisible fingers.*

It was on just such a morning in mid-March that Charlie di Angelis left his bed to jog across the lightly frosted lawns to the school dining room. As usual he had risen at seven forty-five, and as usual he was now hurrying to make breakfast before eight when serving ceased. At seventeen years old, Charlie had already spent three winters trekking through the fog and now gave no thought to it at all.

Joining the listless queue inside the thankfully warm dining room he collected two bowls of cornflakes and a plate of gnarled sausages and tomatoes. He poured a hot mug of tea from the urns, and then, not seeing anyone he knew, took his tray to an empty table.

*It was a Saturday, the last of term. Next Friday he would be on a coach heading back to London. But that still seemed a long way off. Before then, there were at least three way overdue essays to be done and a couple of tests to be prepared for. There was also the fact that he still had to decide where he was going: his mother in London or his father in Florence. Alternatively, of course, there was Luke's offer of a fortnight on the Côte d'Azur on some boat his father had got hold of. This, with reservations, mainly involving the crush Luke was apparently developing for him, he was bearing carefully in mind. It wasn't the crush he minded, so much as the harm to his public image — which reminded him: it was Luke's Millhouse party tonight.*

*Eliot, he noticed, had just entered the dining room in a big ex-army great coat and was staring round rather forlornly. He made for the tea urn, scanning the crowd. As his eye roved towards him, Charlie groaned inwardly. Eliot looked pleased however, and moved his lips in a silent hello.*

*When he had his tea, he came over.*

"Missed last service again," *he grumbled, pulling back a chair and slumping into it.*

"Get an alarm clock." *Charlie suggested.*

"They don't work. I sleep too well." *He eyed Charlie's tray. Charlie noted that Eliot's hair needed a wash and he hadn't shaved.*

"How about lending me one of your bowls of cornflakes?"

"Lending?"

"Yeah, go on."

"No."

"Ah, Jesus!"

"Eliot my dear friend, I need two bowls. Otherwise I get hungry, at about ten o'clock if I have only one bowl. It waits 'till eleven if I have two."

"What waits?"

"The pain in my stomach."

"All right." *Eliot changed tack.* "I'll buy you a cheese roll at break."

*Charlie considered this, trying not to laugh.*

"Two cheese rolls." Eliot said desperately.

"Shit, Eliot. You'll make me nuts. All right."

Eliot quickly reached out for one of the bowls and the milk carton.

" ... Hey, don't finish my milk!"

It was too late. "Charlie," Eliot grunted, crumpling the tetrapak and needlessly dropping it on the floor, "I'll buy you a whole dairy when I'm a millionaire. Stop complaining."

"Millionaire?" Charlie echoed scornfully.

Eliot looked up. "At least." Charlie stared at him and with amazement saw that he was serious. "And how exactly do you intend to manage that?"

Eliot grinned. "Charlie ... " He waved his spoon in the air, sending drops of milk across the table. " ... What did I come into this dining room with? Nothing. What have I got now? The same breakfast you had. Doesn't that tell you anything?" Charlie shook his head. He had no illusions about the cheese rolls. Eliot would have sold his mother for two sausages. But then, the guy made you laugh. What a *contadino*!

Pleased with their respective performances they finished eating and walked down to Assembly together, each enjoying a sense of patronage towards the other. The mist was rising but it was still sharply cool. Charlie decided to share his good news.

"Going to the Millhouse tonight?"

"Might do." Meaning, as Charlie saw immediately he had not been invited. Charlie felt a brief surge of sympathy for the *paysan*. Perhaps he should save the good news. But then again, someone had to get lucky ... and he deserved something for the cornflakes.

"Me too. With Chloe."

Eliot gave him a contemptuous look. "No way."

"Well ... she's asked me to the steam fair at Oldspaine this afternoon. Then we're going on to Luke's together."

Eliot fought to restrain his irritation. So. Chloe was after the wop now. A fact which merely underlined one very significant question. "When was it going to be his turn?"

"She makes my socks look clean," he sneered. Charlie knew jealousy *when he heard it, and rather wished he'd kept his news to himself. But now he felt obliged to say something on Chloe's behalf. "Eliot, the day your socks look clean, the rest of us will have shit in our shoes."*

*Eliot grunted darkly. But Charlie had had enough. "Come on," he said. "Double or quits that cheese roll, bet you the HM gives us another drugs lecture."*

## XXXI

Eliot was not a person to let despondency get the better of him. He had a facility for turning it into anger. Consequently he arrived back at the Millhouse in a spectacularly bad mood. A mood of frustration and fury. Maria had dumped him, Suzanne had played with him, Chloe had insulted him. A little respect was called for, and one of those three, one above all, positively owed it him. He made for the stairs without a backward glance.

Chloe had slept long but fitfully. She was now more than a little aware that coming here was a mistake. It had seemed all right at the time, a country weekend, but at that stage she'd somehow forgotten about the Charlie business. How could she have done that? Anyway, he was back in her mind now. And the quickest way to get rid of him was by a speedy return to London. She woke up hoping she could persuade the others of her point of view.

At that moment, the door flew open and there stood Eliot. She yawned.

He closed the door sharply. "Take your clothes off," he said.

Chloe blinked. "Eliot, you must be sleepwalking. Go back to bed."

"You heard. Get on with it. We've got unfinished business."

"What the *fuck* are you talking about?" She began to sit up, more on the point of laughter than rage.

"Charlie."

"Have you gone fucking mad, uh?"

"Come on." Eliot was out of his pants already. Chloe watched incredulously. "Let me get this right, Eliot. You come in here talking of Charlie and unfinished business, and ask me to take my clothes off?"

"You got it."

Chloe considered this.

"And if I don't?"

"You will."

"For you?"

"Chloe," Eliot sighed, as if dealing with a petulant child, "what you are, actually, is a filthy, selfish, bitch of a whore. We're going to fuck, right now, whether you like it or not."

He came towards her naked. His body was red with heat, strong muscles bulging. His penis was erect.

Eliot tore off the duvet. Chloe was naked except for her white panties. Eliot fixed his eyes on them and plunged. She spun from the bed, breasts swinging, avoiding him by inches. But his hand caught her ankle. "You fucking moron!" she screamed, swinging at him with all her strength. Her fist smacked his ear and his head jerked alarmingly. But like a limpet, he hung on. Chloe was no weakling. She turned, pulled the captured leg in, then kicked. Eliot took it in the face and was half stunned. Chloe lost her balance and crashed backwards. Eliot rolled off the bed half on top of her as she struggled onto her knees. As she twisted she saw blood streaming from his mouth and dripping onto her back. He was gurgling. Then she felt his fingers grab the rim of her underwear and tear downwards, the thin cotton ripping like paper. "You fucking ... " She kicked back again at his bloody mouth. He grabbed her shoulder and yanked. She collapsed onto her stomach. Pinioned and squirming, she felt Eliot climb up her back, and heard his grunt as his cock wedged between her buttocks. She cried out, and swung again. He didn't seem to notice. His forearm slid under her stomach and yanked her up. She felt the exposure of her vagina and tried to wriggle out. He was too strong. And then, quite suddenly, he'd let her go. "All right, bitch," he panted through clenched teeth. "There's something between us, you know what I'm talking about, which makes us *partners* whether you like it or not. Unfinished business, remember?" Chloe suddenly stopped struggling. "Now, do you still want it — or not?"

There was a brief pause.

"You piece of *shit*!" she sneered. But this time, she didn't resist as he reached for her.

## XXXII

*Eliot went to the party. It was true that he had not been invited, an irksome detail which he put down rather to Luke's incompetence than the fact that he owed the latter over a hundred pounds.*

*It was well known, after all, that Luke had money to burn, and in Eliot's view anyone rich enough to hand it out indiscriminately didn't really need to get it back.*

*But then, Luke was, after all, a bit of a dope and allowances had to be made. He concluded that magnanimity was in order as he approached the door of the brightly lit, noisy Millhouse.*

*Bob Marley's hoarse singing voice greeted him as he stepped out of the cold into the smoky kitchen, the thick backbeat reverberating through the house. There were half a dozen people in the immediate vicinity, standing or sitting round a big wooden table. All of them he recognized either from his own year or the one below. Some looked up, but no one bothered to say hello. Eliot closed the door and beamed round at them all anyway. Then he detected the heady aroma of a punch coming from a steaming copper bowl on the Aga and made his way towards it. There were glasses on the table, and as he took one he observed the carcasses of a row of ducks. He felt a pang of irritation. Luke really was out of line not inviting him, especially when he'd been starving all day.*

*He took his glass to the stove and waited for the girl in front to serve herself. He recognized her from the year below, remembered that someone had once said she had a title, but didn't remember her name. She wasn't very attractive however and, he observed, had fat ankles. When she turned to pass the ladle a moment later, she glanced up at his friendly smile without the least flicker of interest. Needled, Eliot served himself and let the ladle slip irretrievably into the hot liquid. Then he moved on to the dining room.*

*Here again, there was more of the same, though the people here seemed less sober than those in the kitchen. This room was the source of the music and a few people were dancing. A bespectacled youth, Ross, with whom he'd shared a study the year before in better days — Moira days — was thumbing drunkenly through the record collection. He was hardly worth greeting, but Eliot decided to wave if he should look up. He didn't.*

*In the sitting room he saw Luke, talking with obvious excitement to Charlie. For a second Eliot's confidence gave way to a moment of alarm. He could technically be asked to leave as a gate-crasher. He was about to back away when Luke glanced up and caught his eye. Eliot grinned instinctively, but Luke showed absolutely no recognition and turned back to Charlie immediately. Eliot relaxed and even wondered if he should go over. But a second look told him that whatever occupied them, it was serious. Charlie was red and looked close to angry, which was for him unusual. Luke, though not apparently drunk, was waving his arms and looking for all the world as though he had something urgent to communicate. Eliot decided to leave them and wandered on to the next room.*

\* \* \*

*Fifteen minutes had passed since Luke had barged in and dragged Charlie off. Chloe was now seriously fed up. She sensed that returning downstairs in an attempt to fetch him might be awkward, but on the other hand the sneaking suspicion that she had been abandoned, combined with the effects of several hours drinking, was making her very angry.*

*She heard footsteps in the hall outside. In rapid succession she got up, smoothed her skirt, sat down again, crossed her legs and fluffed her hair. The footsteps paused outside the door. The door opened, and Eliot appeared.*

*They stared at each other in surprise.* "Hello," *Eliot said at last.* "What are you doing here?"

"Just looking round." *Chloe replied defensively, disconcerted by the fact that he wasn't Charlie.*

"Me too," *Eliot said. There was a pause.* "Pretty boring downstairs, isn't it?"

"Is it?"

"Uh huh. Eliot looked with interest round the room. "Mirrors!" *he said, raising his eyebrows. Chloe shrugged. Suddenly Eliot stepped forward and put a hand on the bed.* "Outstanding," *he said with approval.* "Now that's what I call a bed."

"Have you seen Charlie?" *Chloe asked.*

*Eliot looked up and smiled as if puzzled.* "Charlie?" *he repeated vaguely.* "Oh, Charlie. No I don't ... oh, wait a minute. Yeah. I saw him downstairs."

"What was he doing?" *Chloe demanded, hardly restraining her annoyance. It took Eliot a fraction of a second to gauge the meaning of her tone. He reacted promptly.* "Oh, he's pretty much occupied, if you know what I mean. With Lindsay Duncan." *He straightened up and smirked.* "Nice to see them together again." *Chloe looked up sharply.* "Why?" *Eliot asked casually.* "Were you looking for him?"

"I just wondered where he was."

"Uh huh. Do you mind if I sit down?" *He laughed.* "All this punch-plonk's going to my head." *Chloe didn't respond. He sat about a foot away from her.* "Want some?" *he asked, offering her his glass. Chloe took it, sipped, and handed it back.*

*"What a bed!" Eliot said, delighted. "Wouldn't mind spending a night on this."  He lay back and did not get up. Surreptitiously, he eyed Chloe's back. Then, steeling his nerves, he spoke softly. "You look a little ... glum. Is there anything I can do?"*

*Chloe said nothing and didn't move. Eliot reached out and touched her shoulder. "I'm a good listener," he said earnestly.*

*Downstairs another record had been put on. It could just be identified as the Doors, Jim Morrison singing "Oh show me the way to the next whisky bar ... " A current favourite at Elysia. Eliot edged closer to Chloe and slipped his arm further along her silk-shirted back.*

\* \* \*

*After Charlie had finally left him, Luke went outside and stood for a long time in a daze. The wide glass windows to the indoor swimming pool had been pulled back, and many people in differing states of undress ran past him wet and shrieking. Behind him was laughter and music and the high-pitched drone of half a dozen indistinguishable conversations all vying for prominence. The faces that came running past him were suddenly unfamiliar, bestial. Some stared at him with gargoyle-like intensity, others were contorted in unaccountable excitement. The faces of young people, unused to drink, drunk. Someone shouted at him "Great Party!" but he hardly heard. He was still carrying a glass, he noticed. It slipped from his hand and shattered on the cobbled courtyard.*

*Turning, he stumbled back into the dining room. A boy in spectacles was lying on his back by the record player, gagging. Jim Morrison sang: "Oh show me the way to the next little girl ... " and a chorus of boys and girls with their arms round each other echoed the line a beat out of time.*

*A boy passed eerily by, with a beer bottle apparently glued to his lips. It gave Luke a sudden idea. He must have a drink and forget Charlie's cruel rejection. In a second it was a burning desire leaving him all but paralyzed with thirst. Suddenly panting, he picked his way through the tumbling mass of people to the kitchen. He was heading for the punch, but when he got there the smell told him it would be inadequate. Increasingly exhausted, he retraced his footsteps through the dining room. There were people everywhere. Dozens of them. Had he started this? What madness! As he staggered into the middle of the room a dancing couple literally flew past him, smashing into a standard lamp which exploded with a tinkling of glass. There were shrieks and screams. Luke ignored them all.*

*He could hardly breathe by the time he had negotiated the hall and reached the door to his father's study. He was dimly aware that this awful thirst was a new experience, and under other circumstances might have been concerned by it. But not tonight.*

*There were two people in the study, people he recognized — Suzanne and Martin. He stared at them bitterly.*

*"Excuse me," he said abruptly, and crossed unsteadily to the desk. From the top drawer he pulled out a key and with it opened another drawer below. Flat in the second drawer lay a three-quarter full bottle of Famous Grouse. Luke dragged it out and uncapped it. "I don't suppose there's a glass in here?" He mumbled. Suzanne looked alarmed, but Martin remained still, watching him.*

*"No, well, it doesn't matter." Shakily Luke put the neck of the bottle to his lips and poured.*

*The kick in his gut that cracked his body like a whip did it. It was so good, so right ... to his great relief and surprise it hit him like a revelation: he had found* an answer.

## XXXIII

Luke awoke with a faint but unmistakable hangover and a sense of dread. Suzanne was gone, he noticed. Had she ever been there? He needed a cigarette badly, but he had slipped the carton, he recalled with unusual precision, into Chloe's bag before they'd left London.

Opening the door to her bedroom, Luke was confronted by the incongruous sight of Eliot with a sheet wrapped round his torso, apparently examining his feet. There was dry blood around his mouth. Chloe's form, identifiable only by her blonde hair draped over the side of the bed, was also mummified by cloth. Items of clothing and bedding lay scattered around the bed and its immediate environs.

Eliot looked up in surprise.

"Hello." Luke said.

"Hi." Eliot replied, still looking surprised.

"I'm sorry. I came to get a packet of cigarettes. I think I put the carton in Chloe's bag."

Luke let go of the door handle and walked stiffly towards Chloe's black canvas hold-all.

"You mean," Eliot said with an effort, "that there are cigarettes in that bag? I've been dying for a snout."

"Would you like one?"

"Yep."

Luke unwrapped the packet in his hand. An unfamiliar sensation was carousing unsteadily through his veins, but he wasn't sure what it was. At any rate, his hands seemed very steady, which was unusual.

"That *is* Chloe under there?" Luke said. Eliot nodded.

"Hello." Luke said. "Well, I'll be off then." he handed Eliot two fresh cigarettes from the pack then stopped as the sheet beside Eliot began to rise and the top of Chloe's head, followed by the pale skin of her face, appeared. Luke watched with increasing discomfort.

"Well, well, well." Chloe said, finally risen. "Just fancy, the three of us here together again." There was an odd look in her eyes that Luke didn't like and Eliot wasn't sure about. "Eliot," she said with a frown, "what was it you said before you raped me — partners? Something between just you and me? Didn't you forget someone?" They stared at each other soundlessly for a second, then Chloe put it into words. "All three of us together. Only Charlie's missing now, of course."

## XXXIV

By two o'clock the sun was shining again, though some clouds remained, marbling the sky. Luke had returned from the cellar with an armful of Pouilly fumé and Stolichnaya. He now sat at the kitchen table enjoying a very large glass of the vodka with tonic and lemon. Maria had alternately sat with him and busied herself with the meal. At one point they had gone out together and laid the wooden bench-table combination in the garden. Suzanne had watched them from a deckchair nearby, seated with her own bottle, not offering to help.

It was hot and steamily aromatic in the kitchen now, and Luke felt deeply peculiar. Not only was he in the unusual position of being — except for a few drinks — entirely compos mentis in the face of extraordinarily trying events, but also vague recollections were growing clearer. Like a photograph developing before his eyes, one memory in particular was emerging. It had never really been far away, he realized, though he had subdued it for a long time.

Towards three o'clock Maria said she thought it was about ready and went off to call Chloe and Eliot. In order to occupy himself, Luke got up and opened the wine bottles, at which point he suddenly had what amounted to a vision.

As if in compensation for all the years of self-induced memory loss he saw suddenly, with the greatest clarity, himself, standing by the swimming pool screaming at three familiar figures. He remembered the words. And moments later, without much surprise or emotion, he realized what he had to do.

Maria returned as he was taking the third cork out, followed by Chloe and Eliot. Eliot looked faintly sheepish. Chloe looked disagreeably sulky.

"Are Martin and Suzanne around?" She demanded after casting a challenging glare at Luke from which he did not, to her irritation, avert his eyes.

"Suzanne's sitting in the garden." Maria answered in passing. "I thought we'd eat out there. Martin seems to have disappeared."

"Disappeared?"

"Well, his car's gone."

"Has he argued with Suzanne or something?" Chloe asked curiously. No one answered.

Maria opened the oven door and everyone turned to watch her. The gratin came out sizzling and brown. The salmon followed, wrapped in foil. "That's what I like to see." Eliot contributed. "Once a creature of the deep, now my lunch."

"Would one of you get the plates while I sort out the sauce?" Maria said. Eliot stepped forward.

"Luke, would you mind asking Suzanne to come in, please. We can serve ourselves." Luke went out.

"How did you learn all this cooking?" Chloe asked accusingly.

"I didn't exactly learn. I picked it up, from my mother mostly. It's not hard."

Chloe frowned. Watching her mother cook was not something she remembered. She dropped the subject.

Suzanne came in a minute later with Luke, looking a little steadier. Everyone served themselves and the party drifted outside into the sun.

"Do you have enough?" Maria asked Suzanne once they were all seated. Suzanne nodded at her mostly-empty dish. "Not terribly hungry," she said, and put her sunglasses on.

Eliot had picked up an old newspaper somewhere and was reading it as he came out, snorting with amusement. "Just listen to this," he said incredulously. "Listen: "An unidentified man was yesterday arrested in Stockport, Greater Manchester, after reporting to the police his discovery of a body on local wasteland. He was charged" ... I don't believe this, I just don't ... "He was charged with sodomizing the corpse before reporting its discovery to the police! An unnamed police source described the suspect as, as a 'possible transvestite'." Eliot broke into a raucous guffaw. "My, God, what is this country coming to?"

Chloe picked up her fork. "Look out, the British Emperor's back again," she said.

"Ah, shut up." Eliot said casually.

Chloe did not. "Eliot's problem," she said, "is: he's one hundred years too late. Can't you just picture him in a pith helmet with a riding crop under his arm? he's got all the arrogance, the selfishness, the self-adoration those guys must have had ... "

"Can it." Eliot grunted, but unmoved.

"What *did* happen to the British Empire?" It was Maria. The others looked at her curiously.

"Kind of faded away, dear." Chloe said at last, flatly.

"But *why*?"

There was a pause. Eliot was grinning, aware that this was making Chloe look bad. She said sharply: "When you've got about three hours spare I'll tell you." Then, seeing Eliot's grin: "Anyway, it hasn't gone downhill at all. This country has about the same natural resources as Bangladesh. Why do you think there's a difference in living standards? Because Britain stripped places like Bengal bare one hundred years ago. Yes, Eliot, that's the fun you missed. Imagine: stealing from little brown men while raping their women and all in the name of Empire. Right up your street."

"Bullshit, Chloe. I've never had to rape *anyone*."

"No ... " Maria interrupted. "But ... what I mean, isn't it weird that it's sort of gone into reverse?" Again they looked at her curiously. "I mean it hasn't just gone, we're actually going backwards now; that's what my parents say anyway. Is it true?"

Chloe laughed. "Yeah. Down into the black hole of despond. It'll end with Eliot waving a halberd at the great unwashed as they storm the gates of Buckingham Palace.

"The trouble with you, Chloe," Eliot said easily, "is you think you're so clever you're afraid to take anything seriously ... *I* think Maria just raised a very interesting question."

Chloe started a snort. "Yeah, as in, the Daily Mirror school of apocalypse ... "

Luke cleared his throat. "Excuse me." He was shaking slightly. "I have something to say. Something important." The eating stopped. Everyone looked round.

Luke fixed Chloe with an unsteady eye and said, "Chloe Mills, I have to... I have something to... I want to tell you something. You are ... really... scum. That's it. Thank you." He looked down at his plate and picked up his cutlery.

Chloe looked at Eliot, then back at Luke. Her eyes narrowed. "You know," she said slowly, "I am having a very weird morning. A positively *surreal* morning. First Eliot the brainless clod barges into my room and attempts to rape me. And now, in the midst of a *particularly* moronic conversation, the Drip of the Year, King Sodden himself, starts insulting me for no reason. What have I done to deserve this? Am I unwittingly wearing my "Piss on Chloe" hat today? No, I think not." She leant forward abruptly. "So, perhaps if it's not too much trouble, Luke, you'd care to explain what you just said."

Luke's nervousness was apparent in the way his hands shook. "Just what I said." He muttered, eyes down. Chloe laughed. "You know Luke, maybe you should lay off those ego-boosting drugs. If you're on about this morning, I repeat, I wasn't in bed with Eliot out of choice. Apart, of course, from the fact that I got fuck all out of you.

"No." Luke said, spitting some food out, his voice suddenly rising, broken by tension. "You know what I mean. And I wanted to tell you this a long time ago. I'd forgotten ... well, not exactly forgotten, I made myself unable to remember." Luke slowly looked up into Chloe's eyes and enunciated his words very carefully. He repeated:

"You are *a slut*."

Chloe's mouth fell open. She recovered quickly. "Luke, you're either stoned or mad. I'm not going to trade insults with you, because I'd cut you into little pieces before you could say "junkie". I'm your guest, and I owe you that."

"That didn't stop you last time."

"What?"

"Charlie died on account of you." Luke's voice and lip were trembling.

Silence fell. Chloe went red. Eliot tried to intercede. "Hey, Luke, slow down ... " he murmured aghast.

Luke went on in a shaky voice. "All I know is, you went to bed with Eliot because you couldn't even wait for Charlie to come back to you. If you'd just waited, ten, fifteen minutes, it wouldn't have happened. That's all." Suzanne leaned forward on her elbows, balancing her glass precariously in front of her lips, looking faintly interested.

"What the *fuck*, Luke, are you talking about?"

Luke nodded deliberately. His whole body was quivering. "I should have said something at the time. But I was scared of you. I'm still scared of you. Five years I've been hiding, but some things ... fifteen minutes. But that was too long for you to wait. That's what I'm talking about."

Chloe looked incredulous. She stared at her adversary for a long moment. No one else had eaten, or spoken. "Well, Luke," she breathed at last. "Behind that glazed, braindead ... squishy exterior there beats a bleeding heart."

Luke suddenly shrank. The moment was over. "I cared about him," he said. "I cared about him ... " His voice tailed away.

Chloe leant slowly backwards, shaking her head in mock disbelief.

"Oh, you slay me Luke."

Luke was beginning to crumple, drained. Tears were flowing from his eyes, he began to sob.

"You poor fool." Chloe went on slowly. "Do you want to know about your friend, Mr Charlie di Angelis, you want to hear what an Angel he *really* was compared to me, the slut? You know where he went after you that night? Straight into the arms of Lindsay Duncan. Jesus, *he* was the one who couldn't wait ten minutes!"

"You fucking *liar* ... ! "

"Well, come on now," Eliot said anxiously. "This is all past history. Why don't we just talk about something — economics, that was interest ..."

"Jesus. I'm not lying. I remember Eliot telling me quite clearly ... " Her voice broke off in mid-sentence. Slowly she turned to Eliot. Luke went white as a sheet and stopped stock still.

Eliot made a blustery noise. "Christ," he said, "how do you guys remember all this? It's years ago ... "

"I remember it very well." Chloe said sharply. She looked from Eliot back to Luke. Luke was staring open-mouthed at Eliot. Eliot had turned a bright red.

Suddenly, Luke rose to his feet. He stood perfectly still for a second, his face white and tear-stained, staring with some strange unfathomable emotion at Eliot. Then he groaned, put his hands to his head, and stumbled away from the table.

They watched him go.

Chloe said slowly, "Was that my imagination, or did it really happen?"

Suzanne got up. "I think I'll go for a walk too," she said in a whisper.

Chloe turned violently towards her. "No comment as usual, Suzanne? And what about *your* murky little business? Why don't you tell us why Elysia closed down, so we can really wallow in it?"

Suzanne turned, stared intently at Chloe, and said: "Because you really wouldn't understand my murky little business, Chloe." and turned away.

"This is ridiculous." Eliot said loudly.

Chloe turned to him "Why don't *you* just shut the fuck up?"

"What actually happened?" It was Maria.

Chloe turned slowly and stared at her for a long time. It was obvious she had no intention of answering. "Please." Maria said.

"There was an accident." Chloe said at last.

She seemed to reflect for a while. Then she said: "Somebody put us down here in this earthly paradise. We should've come out ready to rule the world. But something went wrong. Maybe it was the system, maybe it was us. And some people never got over it. That's all that happened."

## XXXV

*It wasn't much of an impulse, but it counted. One of the things Chloe liked about Charlie was his good cheer. To see him so painfully distraught, as just now when he'd stepped in and found Eliot on top of her, struck a chord somewhere. Like, something was wrong. She pulled away from Eliot. "Hey. OK, let go ... "*

*"I can't, Chloe, I can't stop now ... "*

*"Get fucking* off!*" And then, to move him: "We'll finish this later."*

*And before Eliot could get a word out, she'd wriggled out, was rebuttoning her blouse and was on her way to the door.*

*There was an argument going on by the pool. The French windows were open to the summer evening, and two people were arguing on the threshold. She could tell by their voices it was Luke and Charlie.*

*She approached by the courtyard, and saw with surprise that it was empty. Then she realized that it had just passed ten o'clock — the magic hour for those without exeats. Most of them had had to go back to school.*

*Luke had a bottle in his hand. He was waving it in front of Charlie, who appeared to be crying. Charlie said, "Luke, please, leave me alone? I don't want your help, I don't want your sympathy. And you're fucking drunk."*

*Then she heard Eliot's voice behind her: "Hey, Chloe, wait a minute ... "*

Chloe ignored it and went up to the boys. "Everything all right?" she asked.

"Oh, great!" Luke shouted. "You should know!"

Chloe spoke to Charlie "What is this?"

"Nothing," Charlie muttered.

"Charming. In that case I think I'll just go back to bed."

"Not in my house, you slut — I've heard about you and Eliot!"

*Luke was shaking with rage. Chloe turned slowly, her face suffusing.*

"Luke, don't call her that!" Eliot's voice came from behind.

"Fuck you, Eliot," Charlie rang out. "Why don't you and your rotten whore just keep out of it!"

Somehow, this incensed Luke. "Yeah, well you ... you ... you can just both shut-up and get out of my ... "

"How dare you!" It was Chloe, her voice so low that they all turned to look at her. She was shaking with rage. "How dare you call me slut? Whore? I am the one fucking woman in this place who's not a hypocritical bitch, who doesn't lead you on. And you call me those things. You moronic, ignorant ... "

" ... Then what are you?" Luke yelled furiously. If slut isn't the word for you what is?" There was a brief silence.

"Oh, Luke, Stop it. You're being a fucking drunken arsehole." It was Charlie.

Luke turned, swung the bottle, not very threateningly; but as Charlie retreated he slipped on a puddle of water and fell backwards. It ought to have been funny. He made a comic noise, a Who, oh, ooh! and fell into the pool, arms windmilling. His head clipped the adjacent side of the pool with a little "thok" sound. "Serves you right." Luke cried, tears flooding down his cheeks. "You're all bastards, all of you! Just fuck off, all of you!" And he stumbled off across the courtyard.

"Come on, Chlo ... " Eliot wheedled. "Let's go back ... "

"Forget it Eliot. I've had enough. Of all of you."

*"But you said ... "*

*"I said forget it, arsehole, can't you hear?"*

Eliot went red, as she turned on her heel. "Well, aren't you going to help your beloved out?" he shouted after her sarcastically, belatedly noticing that Charlie was floating on his face in the water. Chloe turned for a second. She looked at the swimming pool, then at Eliot. "You help him. He's not my beloved, not by a long chalk."

"Well he's more yours than fucking mine." Eliot exploded. They stared at each other.

*In that fraction of a second, something passed between them, that neither could have explained.*

*They turned away simultaneously.*

## XXXVI

Suzanne was half way down the drive before she saw the car coming towards her. Since the lane was confined by a barbed wire fence on either side there was no escape. She edged over to let it pass and continued on her way with a firm step.

As she half expected, the car slowed as it approached. But before Martin could open his window she was past, increasing her pace.

He opened the door and climbed out. "Hey, Suzanne," he called after her. She did not stop.

Reaching inside, he switched off the engine off then jogged after her, slowing only when he was alongside.

"Come on, Suzanne," he said.

"I thought you'd gone." She was still walking fast and not looking at him.

"I just went for a drive, that's all. Where are you going?"

Suzanne did not answer. Martin thrust his hands deep in the pockets of his coat. "Suzanne ..."

"Martin, I don't want to talk. I want to be alone."

"Suzanne ... " Martin drew a deep breath. "Come on. Stop a minute. I need to talk to you. I told you I was in trouble.

"Then why talk to me?" Suzanne's tone was flat. "I haven't seen you for five years, Martin. When I last saw you I thought I mentioned that I never wanted to see you again. That hasn't changed."

"Then I'll ask you again, why'd you come down?"

"I didn't know you'd be here."

"Yeah. You came for the other good company. OK, let's try something different. What is the problem?"

"You just don't get it do you?"

"That's true."

"I *loved* you Martin. I loved you." She took a step towards him, and he saw that there were tears in her eyes. Her voice broke. "You were the *one* ... how do you explain love to someone like you? You'll *never* get it, Martin, because you'll never understand love, you useless, stupid ... " She ran at him and hit out at his chest with balled fists. Stunned, Martin tried to put his arms around her. She pulled away violently, and stumbled.

"Suzanne," he muttered, trying to help her up from the track. "Jesus, Suzanne, you are so beautiful. Still. Always were, always ..."

She shied away as if he were poisonous. As soon as she was on her feet she began to run, absurdly twisted, with her face in her hands. "Wait. *Please*." He ran after her, caught her, grabbed her by the shoulders and spun her round. She swung her face away from him. "Look," he said. "Suzanne, I am *not* a monster. I swear it. And whatever I am, I want to change anyway." She seemed to be studying his face through her tears, but was struggling less. He went on: "Suzanne, I never forgave myself for what happened with you. I did a bad thing. But I've known it and regretted it for five years. And I never stopped missing you. Your beauty." He wished tears would come, to help him. "Suzanne, you were the one for me, too. You were and you are. I'm asking you to help me put this one last thing out of the way. If you help me I know I can do it, and then maybe we can ... just give me a *chance*, Suzanne. Suzanne, I loved you and I love you."

She made a sudden noise of disgust, jerked away as hard as she could, and surprised by the intensity of the fury in her eyes he released her. "You think I'm beautiful?" Her voice was low and ugly. She staggered a step away from him. "Beautiful ... " The word, repeated, seemed to have a calming effect on her. She turned to Martin slowly, and spoke almost dreamily. "Remember the stars, Martin? Would you travel out to them if you could, even if you found yourself in hell instead of heaven? Would you still, Martin?"

He could not speak.

"Well, Martin. Let me tell you about how beautiful I am. I'm about as beautiful as you. I've got the big one, Martin, the big one ... from needles, probably." She waited until his confused look vanished. "*That's* why I came down, to show you me. You're just too fucking late, Martin. And even if you weren't, I have no feelings now, except absolute hatred. For you, and for me too, but mostly for you. That is my only motivating force now, and that is why I came here to see you. I want you to have this memory." She planted her legs apart, still staggering slightly, and raised her arms, star-fashion. "Of this! Of this disease-ridden corpse you created."

She watched him for a further second. There were tears in her eyes, but she smiled. "So, it's happened. For once, I get to leave you without an answer." She lowered her arms, seemingly exhausted, and slowly turned away again. He did not attempt to stop her.

## XXXVII

*A sixteen-year old named Björn was caught in his second term at Elysia, wandering around the reservoir above the school singing his country's national anthem. It was one o'clock in the morning and he had woken a teacher who lived nearby; when the teacher approached, Björn pulled out a Bowie knife, brandished it, then fell flat on his face in a dead faint. A small plastic envelope found in his wallet contained a suspicious-looking white powder.*

*Events like this were irregular but not unknown at Elysia. At least once or twice a year an irredeemably wild teenager slipped through the undemanding entrance procedure; in most cases he (or sometimes she) would be pushed unwillingly through by desperate parents, loath to admit their child's abnormality and do something sensible about it but happy to pay for an unending succession of schools across Europe for the sake of appearances. With its reputation for high fees and progressiveness, Elysia often formed a link in these chains.*

*In most instances, a recognizable pattern of events would unfold. First, the newcomer would attract attention and even popularity amongst his peers by his uncompromising individuality. He might be recklessly rude to teachers, and be admired for it. But after a while, he would go too far and play his jokes indiscriminately on teachers and pupils alike. His new friends would abandon him, and teachers would start looking for an excuse to dispatch the trouble-maker. Painfully ostracized, the child would be goaded (or resort) to some extremity of behaviour, be caught, and to the relief of everyone (except his parents) be asked to leave.*

\* \* \*

*It happened to be a Saturday, and after a couple of classes in the morning Martin had a free day ahead. Normally he would have spent it with Suzanne, but she had grown conscientious and was working hard for her A-Levels.*

*Martin was well aware that school was drawing to a close. A decision on his future was called for. College was unappealing, as was regular work. The only interesting option, if it could be called that, was Alex's proposition.*

*Suzanne's brother Alex had been taking the two of them out, recently. He called it combining business with pleasure, though his business was never specified. Then one Saturday Suzanne had had the flu. Alex rang to say that he was in Bournemouth as usual, why didn't Martin join him anyway. Martin had agreed.*

*In Alex's hotel suite that July afternoon, Martin observed his first major drugs transaction. When the three young Asians had left, Alex poured two glasses of champagne and took Martin out onto the balcony. He was an athletic-looking man, with a peculiar hardness in his eyes which had always impressed Martin.*

*"Know how I started doing this?" he asked. "When I was fourteen I saw the film "Midnight Express". I was on school holiday in Bogota. The next time I came back to Elysia I carried five grammes of coke. The film scared the shit out of me. That's why I did it. Understand that?"*

*Martin said nothing. Alex cast his eyes over the beach below. "Something tells me you can. I have a feel for people." His eyes roamed* restlessly. "Listen: you heard about the Black Dragon business at Elysia? I was there. Two girls disappeared. We never found out what happened to them. One of them I knew well." There was silence until he shook his head. "After that, I saw the truth. There's you, and there's the rest of the world; there's winners and losers. That's it, Martin, that's all. And I'm winning, Martin. That's a simple fact. I've got a good client base with plenty of cash and, for the moment at least, limited competition. I made two and a half million in the last six months, and that's not even peanuts. There are billions out there. But the trouble is, the bigger I get, the more I need people. And who can I trust? And who can I trust and know they're not stupid? That's a tough one."

Alex had then more or less made him a proposition. And the more Martin thought about it, the more interested he became.

The first intimation he had that something was wrong was when he walked into Guinevere, Suzanne's house. She wasn't in her study, and when he asked a normally loquacious friend of hers, she was unnaturally evasive. Martin went back to his study and found three teachers standing in the midst of a newly-created chaos.

As soon as he entered one of them said "You, come with me." and grabbed his shoulder. Martin shook him off, but the other two jumped in and took his arms. Martin struggled for a second, then stopped. They took him in silence down the corridor, out into the courtyard across to where the headmaster's house stood independent of the school. In the hall one of them said: "Which room is best?"

There was a moment's hesitation. "Well ... a bedroom?" The men bundled him up the stairs. On the landing they waited again while one of them looked into the rooms. "I suppose he can go in there ... ? " He was pushed through. The teachers followed, releasing him for the first time, all panting. One of them shut the door behind him.

Martin looked at them. One was the gym teacher, the other two taught maths and geography. He'd had lessons with all three of them.

He began to rise. "Would someone mind telling me ... " The gym teacher stepped forward, grabbed him by the lapels of his coat and pushed him back, hard. He fell back on the bed. "You filthy little vermin," the teacher hissed. Martin didn't try again.

They stayed there for a ridiculously long time, over an hour. It was a child's bedroom, with painted ships on the wallpaper. Martin couldn't concentrate for the first half hour. Then, slowly, he began to calculate.

The headmaster appeared eventually, red-faced and sweating slightly. He was a tall, bird-like man with craggy features, neatly dressed. Martin was still on the bed. The four men stood looking at him for several long seconds. Finally the headmaster shook his head. He spoke in a slow, measured voice: "You were given opportunities most children would beg for. Privileges. Advantages. And not only have you thrown that ... wealth of opportunity away. You have corrupted others. You have descended to a level where I can only see you with disgust. And anger, and bitterness. You have taken advantage of a system which has cosseted you. You have sold drugs in my school."

Martin did not respond.

"You will give me the names of the people you have sold drugs to. And the name of anyone else in this House who has sold drugs. Now."

Martin murmured something.

"What?"

"I'm not with you."

The headmaster shook his head sadly. "The boy I expelled yesterday said you provided him with cocaine. And we have already found these in your study." He held up two sachets. Martin was silent for a second, then shrugged.

"And?"

For a moment the headmaster did not understand. Then he narrowed his eyes. "This is not a joke. This is far from that. I asked for names."

Martin shrugged again. "How many names do you want? Five? Ten? ... fifty?" The headmaster blinked.

"Expel me and you can read the names in any newspaper that'll listen.

This place already has the Black Dragon to its name. I could get it closed down without even trying."

"He's bluffing." The gym teacher said.

The headmaster raised a hand. "Leave us alone a moment," he said without turning. The three teachers hesitated, then left, closing the door.

Martin and the headmaster stared at each other. Then the headmaster moved to the only chair in the room and sat down. He moved as he spoke, ponderously. But his eyes remained sharp.

"You must," he said quietly, "have been about fourteen when I became headmaster here. You must have known — by sight at least — some of those people. People involved in the incident you refer to as the Black Dragon."

Martin didn't answer.

"You probably also recall my predecessor here, Robinson Rutter. Well, I shall be frank. Dr Rutter was a brilliant man, but he had the misfortune to lose his way. That is no secret today. And pupils — barely more than children — died in that wretched business. To this day, two bodies remain unrecovered. And when you look at it carefully, it was all because Dr Rutter allowed things to get out of hand." He shook his head. "It would be a crime, nothing less than a crime, if I were to do the same. Therefore, I will be ruthless, if necessary, for the greater good. I hope you understand that." He sighed, a note of exasperation entering his tone. "I want names. I do not particularly want you blabbing to newspapers. And I don't think you will do, because not even someone of your standards, I hope, would wish to see a friend's life ruined along with your own. I want you to know that Suzanne Baez is also here in this house now. It appears to me that she is involved in this too. We also found drugs in her study. However, I am prepared to accept that they were yours, left there inadvertently. But if I am to believe this, I will need to see your good faith demonstrated. That means names."

Alex was momentarily surprised and impressed.

"You are lying ... and blackmailing me."

"I can only assure you that I am entirely serious. And do not presume to take a moral position with me young man. Everything I do is for a greater good. You..." he stood up. " ... you on the other hand, and your sordid drug-dealing, are incomprehensible to me."

"Look, Headmaster. Please listen. Listen carefully. I haven't done you any harm, don't try to do me any. You'll regret it if you do. If you want me to leave, I'll leave; for everything else you've just said, let's both forget it right here."

The headmaster looked at him blankly.

"Suzanne has done nothing wrong and you know it." Martin said. "You know that. And she has the right to finish school."

The headmaster shook his head again. "Perhaps you misled the girl. Perhaps she misled you. Perhaps you will both learn something this way." He turned to the door and took the handle. "You will stay in my house tonight. In the morning you will be given one more chance. Otherwise I will inform your and her parents and have both of you driven to the train station. I repeat: I want names." He left the room silently. Martin heard the key turn in the lock.

\* \* \*

Several hours later, Martin crept from his bed and opened the window. The bedroom was on the second floor, there was no way down but to jump. He jumped, rolled and got to his feet. Nothing was broken. He crept back into the main school, entered his study and retrieved a camera. Then he returned to the headmaster's house and went in through its unlocked front door. He found the kitchen and rifled through the drawers until he found a steak knife. Then he soundlessly mounted the stairs as far as the bedroom he had been held in. Two doors down was the room outside which he had earlier heard the headmaster speaking to Suzanne. She had been crying.

He turned the key, and entered silently. He whispered her name into the darkness. Then he closed the door and switched on the light.

Suzanne was on her stomach, her face buried in the pillow. When she *looked up, she didn't even seem to recognize him. Her face was bloated with tears, ugly. He went to her and sat down. "Martin ... " She whispered. "What happened? What's happening? This'll kill my father. It'll kill him!" Her voice began to rise. Martin made soothing noises. "It's OK." he said. "I promise you. Nothing's going to happen. Tomorrow everything's back to normal. I promise you."*

*She looked at him with desperate hope. He nodded. "OK," he said. "Here's what we're going to do ... "*

*"No," she said when he finished. "No."*

*"It's the only way. Otherwise they'll hurt you."*

*Her eyes were frightened, disbelieving. "No! No. I can't do that ... "*

*"You have to. It's us or them."*

*"Martin, if I do it I'll die ... "*

*"Well, it's not just you, Suzanne, it's your Dad like you said. And let's face it, if that happened, Alex'd probably kill the HM. Literally. So think of it as if we're doing him a favour."*

*"I can't. There must be another way ... "*

*Martin sat back. He waited until her breathing had slowed, then spoke softly. "Suzanne, trust me."*

*Suzanne waited outside while Martin entered the headmaster's bedroom. He approached the bed silently, and knelt down beside the man. He was sleeping on his side. Martin put the knife across his neck and pressed. The headmaster's eyes opened, widened, and he tried to rise. The knife bit into him and he fell back. Martin's face was centimetres away. He said: "The thing you must realize here, is that I am really, really serious." With his free hand he pressed a rolled up handkerchief into the man's mouth.*

*Suzanne came in, and Martin had her blindfold the man first; then, always keeping the knife to his throat, had her remove his pyjamas. Using socks, Suzanne tied his arms and legs to the bedposts. Martin checked the knots, then turned the lights on. The man was trembling slightly.*

*"OK." Martin said. "Suzanne, let's go."*

*With tears pouring from her eyes, Suzanne began to undress. At one* point Martin touched her shoulder, but she pulled away from him. When she was naked, Martin removed the headmaster's blindfold.

He looked round with a mixture of fear and fury — and amazement when he saw Suzanne naked. Martin already had the camera to his eye. He motioned to Suzanne, who approached the bed. She stopped when the man began to struggle violently. She turned to Martin. He said: "It'll be over in two minutes. Trust me." She climbed onto the bed, and astride the man's legs. The flash on the camera burned. Martin circled the bed, taking shots. The bulb popped. The headmaster made a noise like an animal through his gag. Suzanne knelt on his legs, sobbing quietly. Martin said: "OK. I want you to imagine, Doctor Wolff, that you're having breakfast. Reading the paper. You see these pictures, hazy with bits blacked out, but there's no mistaking what they are. And you read the article. It's one of your colleagues from the Headmaster's Conference, one of the smart progressive schools; reserved sort of guy, bachelor, wife died a few years back. His story is, he expelled these two kids and locked them in his house overnight. He says that's standard procedure. He woke up with a knife at his throat and the kids tied him up and took these pictures. But the girl says she offered to have sex with him if he'd reconsider, and he agreed. She even agreed to cater for his special needs. But then she released her boyfriend, who burst in and took pictures. At that point the headmaster struggled, of course. OK, Suzanne. Take the gag out of his mouth and get off him." He continued to take pictures. The headmaster fell back, exhausted. "Now," Martin went on. "Who do you believe? Maybe either side. But let me ask you another question. Do you really still want this guy in your cosy club? Would you ever seriously trust him again after that?" He nodded to Suzanne. She left the room, holding her clothes in front of her. Martin lowered the camera, sat down on the bed beside the headmaster, lowered his head and stared into his glazed eyes. He felt a sudden burning elation, a sense of victory and invincibility. He smiled at the headmaster until he was forced to see it too. "So, Dr Wolff... I'm going to untie you now, then Suzanne and I are going back to my study. You do exactly as you like. But my suggestion is that we get up tomorrow and all *pretend the last twelve hours never happened."*

\* \* \*

*The next day, Martin and Suzanne were back in their old studies. No announcement had been made about their leaving, and none was made about their return. Rumours spread like wildfire, and everyone knew that something extraordinary had happened. Martin wasn't talking about it however, and Suzanne wasn't talking at all. Mysteriously, she seemed to withdraw completely into herself during her last month at Elysia. Martin was seen with her once or twice, but she was clearly unhappy in his company. She turned up to few meals and it was even rumoured that she had anorexia as she became thinner. That summer she took poor A-Levels, then disappeared entirely, keeping in touch with no one and leaving no clue where she was going.*

*A short time later the headmaster called a meeting of the governors and announced his resignation. While a replacement was sought, an unbalanced youth tried to blow up a sports pavilion with a homemade fertilizer bomb, severely injuring himself in the process. Miraculously, he survived; but this time the school did not. In the aftermath a private offer was made for the premises. At the end of the following academic year, the school closed down.*

*Four years later Suzanne happened to meet Chloe at a London party. They had never been friends at school, but the moody blonde now seemed to strike some kind of a chord in Suzanne. Shortly afterwards, Chloe left her father's home in Chelsea and moved into her flat.*

## XXXVIII

Suzanne doubled back via the river after a short time. She wasn't sure what was going to happen next, and wasn't sure she cared. She wanted to go home. She'd forgotten how quiet this part of the world could be, and now she hated it.

She was surprised when she found Luke in her path as she neared the Millhouse. He was sitting as a fisherman might sit if he had been there all day, slumped with his chin on his chest. But there was no fishing rod, and he stirred as he heard her approach

She stopped, and for a second they both stared at each other. "I'm sorry," Suzanne heard herself say, "about Charlie." Luke pursed his lips and made the usual shrugging gesture that had become second nature. "It's all right," he said. "We never even did anything together. It was just ... a school thing. Stupid."

Suzanne took a step or two further down the path, then stopped and turned back. Slowly she eased herself into a sitting position beside him. He averted his eyes and stared blankly at the river. After a while he realized that she was silently crying. He leant forward and was sick into the river.

"Sorry." He said. "You know, first I blamed myself. Then Chloe. Then I forgot, mostly. Then it came back, you saw ... and now I have to blame Eliot ... but I can't start hating him now, it's too crazy."

Suzanne shook her head, still crying. Luke felt water in his eyes, and started to cry too. He reached out his hand, and she held it. She looked much younger. Like a child. "You know," Luke said, "I have this dream sometimes ... "

"Don't ... talk."

Rain began to fall, but neither of them moved.

\* \* \*

"You know," Eliot said, "all this shit is really getting me down. I mean, what is the point, dredging it up now? I'm fucked if I'm going to let it put me off my lunch. I'm going to get some fresh." He stood up and glared challengingly at Chloe. "You want some?"

"You're a bastard, Eliot," she said.

"For what?" He laughed. "For not blaming myself over Charlie? Bullshit."

"He died."

"Years ago!" Eliot exclaimed in a strangled voice. "Listen, if you hadn't had your eye on him, it might not have happened either. But it did. Jesus! What are we supposed to do? Prosecute each other? I liked him too, but he does not exist any more. That's it."

Chloe sat several seconds staring at him expressionlessly. "You're a bastard, Eliot," she said drily. She picked up her plate and handed it to him. Eliot's lips curled into a small, tight grin.

\* \* \*

Martin met Maria in the kitchen, where she was clearing up. He came in, went to the fridge and pulled out a carton of milk, from which he drank thirstily.

"Do you want some lunch?" she asked. He turned. "Thanks. No."

Maria sighed, looking at the dishes on the table. She moved to some cupboards, and opened them in turn until she found a roll of foil. Martin watched her.

"Is something wrong?" she asked.

"Nothing that matters."

"The others thought you'd left this morning. I thought you'd come back."

"Really."

"For Suzanne."

"What made you think that?"

"You still love her, don't you?"

Martin was silent.

"I could see it."

Martin put down the milk and moved towards the door. "Thanks for the offer of lunch." As he reached the door Eliot came through it. They stared at each other for a second. Then Eliot turned to Maria waving his plate. "This kind of got cold. Chloe and me, we'll start over."

"Good!" Maria responded. "I thought we'd have to throw it away." Eliot turned to Martin. "You're back," he said warily. For some reason, Martin didn't look as formidable as usual. At the same time, Eliot discovered that he was feeling peculiarly assertive himself. A general uncertainty about Martin flowered in that moment into a deep dislike.

"Eliot," Martin said, following him back in, "I wonder if I could have a word ... "

"Yeah, what?"

"Well ... " Martin broke off. Luke and Suzanne had come through the door. They were holding hands, and slightly wet. Luke said: "It's raining." A second later, Chloe came past them.

"Look ... " Martin interrupted. "Since you're all in one place, maybe I can just have a second ... ? "

"Christ," Chloe said, apparently not hearing him. "Why don't we have something to drink instead of just standing around." She looked round,

155

avoiding Luke's eye.

"Good idea." Eliot said aggressively. "This throat is definitely open for business."

"There's some bottles under the table." Maria said. Chloe went to have a look.

Martin spoke. "I just wanted to say, I'm in a bit of trouble. I need someone to help me out ... you all know me, so you can guess what I'm talking about." He paused. No one moved. "I don't think there's too much risk. Anyway, I'd make it worth your while." He looked round at the assembled faces. "I know how you feel Suzanne." He met Chloe's eyes, but she frowned and looked away confused.

"Luke?" Luke opened his eyes wide. "Well, I'd like to help, Mart. But I'd fuck it up. I just haven't got it in me."

"Eliot?"

"Trouble." Eliot smiled. Martin interpreted his grin too quickly. "This is worth a lot to me, Eliot."

Eliot's grin slid away. "I don't need your fucking money." Martin said quickly: "All right. You can take some coke if that suits you better ... "

Eliot's eyes flickered and he looked hesitant. He glanced at Maria, who looked away; and at Chloe, who did the same. His face congealed into a haughty sneer.

"No," he said. "I'm not that interested, actually."

All their eyes were on Martin. He seemed to have nothing else to say.

Maria said: "I'll do it."

Suzanne whispered "Don't ... "

Martin looked at her. He said: "I'd appreciate it. I'll explain later."

He turned to go, then stopped. "By the way. They found the bodies. The Black Dragon bodies. They arrested someone in Stockport and found Heather Cloate's diaries in his house. It was on the radio this morning."

"Who?"

"No one knows yet. The radio said he was a transvestite. It'll come."

## XXXIX

Shortly after six o'clock Martin pulled off the motorway into a Sussex village consisting of a number of gabled cottages along two adjoining lanes, a pub named "The Freemason's Arms", and a duckpond at the intersection of the two lanes. About a mile outside this village, by a gated drive, he parked and got out. Opening the boot, he took out the video camera, gave it to Maria and spoke briefly. Maria then walked away. Martin got back into his vehicle and took a small silenced Heckler and Koch and ammunition from the glove compartment. He removed the magazine and put in three blanks, then three bullets, so that the bullets would be fired first. A moment later he changed his mind and replaced the blanks with bullets.

After careful surveillance of his target, Martin knocked at the front door of the Georgian house at the end of the drive. After a long pause, an ageing man of about seventy in a threadbare tweed jacket appeared and looked at him with unfocusing suspicion.

"Good evening," Martin said. "I'd like to speak to Sir Michael."

"Got an appointment?" the old man croaked.

"No. Just tell him I'm a friend of his daughter Nadeine. And it's very important."

"Wait here." With what seemed like considerable effort, the old man raised his eyebrows skeptically and returned inside, shutting the door on him. Martin took out the pistol and held it behind his back.

Two minutes later, the door was reopened, this time by a younger man in his early fifties. He had sharp dark eyes, a tanned, slightly bullish face, and an impatient frown. He stared at Martin. "I don't know you."

"No."

"Well?"

"What?"

"My name is Martin." The man seemed to ponder for a moment. Then started and blinked several times rapidly. Then Martin pointed the gun at him. He froze. "What do you want?"

"I just want a word, off the record. I won't even come in your house."

The man looked belligerent for half a second, then afraid again. He spoke in a stumbling voice. "I don't know who you are, I've never seen you before in my life, and you're threatening me. What the hell do you want?" With his free hand Martin pulled some Polaroids from his pocket.

"I'd like to know what connection you have with this police operation. I took these in Wiltshire this morning."

"I haven't a clue what you mean."

"The van in that picture is a police car. That man is a policeman. All right. Two possibilities. I want to know which is right: A, you got wind that Nadeine was seeing someone not altogether suitable for the daughter of someone in your position. So you used your influence to try and get me arrested. B, you used your influence to the same end, but Nadeine persuaded you to do it. Before you deny it, you should know that Nadeine was the only person I told I'd be in Wiltshire."

The man gathered himself to speak with authority. "Look. This is all nonsense and I have no idea what you're talking about." He hesitated. "All I know is, if you're in trouble you still appear to have a good chance of getting away. But if you hurt me, you won't stand a chance."

"I'm not here for revenge. I just want the facts. It's loaded." He turned to the drive and fired off three silent shots in quick succession. Gravel spurted. The man jumped. Martin took his finger off the trigger, broke open the magazine to show that there were bullets there, and held it out to him. "Good faith," he said.

Amazed, the man took the gun gingerly. He fumbled as he pointed it at Martin, then said: "You're mad. I'm going to telephone the police."

"Your lines are cut."

"Then we'll drive to them." Almost as an afterthought he prodded the gun forward. "Put your hands up." Cautiously, he leaned forward and patted Martin's coat a few times. Finding nothing, he shook his head in disbelief. "My daughter was right. You're not just a blackmailer, you're mad."

"Blackmailer?"

The man was now elated by his triumph. "What did you have in mind? "MEP's daughter in drug orgy"? You paltry creature. Do you think I'm too afraid of *that* to turn you in?"

Martin said wearily: "I doubt it, since it wouldn't really affect you."

The man looked momentarily confused.

"Sir Michael, are you blind? There was no blackmail. Nadeine just wanted money. She's cursing you right now for going to the police instead of coming up with it. That is what she said, isn't it? You were to give *her* the money before she gave it to me?"

The man blinked. "That's enough," he snapped. "Come with ... "

Martin slowly lowered his arms until they were by his sides. The man yelped apoplectically: "Put your bloody hands back up, now!"

"What are you going to do? Shoot me?"

"Don't tempt me."

Martin looked straight at him. "Here's one good reason why you shouldn't. I've fixed it so Nadeine will be busted tonight. No big deal, but if anything happens to me here ... " he shrugged. "Drug dealer shot by MEP, daughter was customer?" Now *that* you could find sticky."

"You think I believe that?"

"That Nadeine's going down? Do you think I'd give you my gun without covering myself? Come on; what did she tell you? That she "tried it, just once"? She's an addict. She must've asked you for cash enough times. This whole thing was a scam. It didn't work out, and I was expendable. It's that simple."

The man blinked rapidly.

"Now," Martin said, "I'm going to turn round and walk away."

Beads of sweat were breaking out on his adversary's forehead. Martin met his gaze and held it, then turned to the place where the drive curled out of sight into the woods. He turned and began to walk.

"Stop!" the man bellowed.

Martin fixed his eyes on a tree at the mouth of the drive and doggedly went towards it. He thought he'd won, but it didn't stop the fear. The man aimed the gun at the middle of Martin's back, his finger tightened on the trigger, then he relaxed. Martin disappeared round the corner of the drive.

A minute later Martin picked up his car and drove back to the road. He turned right, away from the village and pulled over after about half a mile. He turned the engine off and reached for the car phone. After some delay, Pascual's careful voice came on the line.

"Put me through to Alex, Pascual."

"Still not back, Martin. Sorry."

"Tell him my problem is solved. Tell him now." There was a pause. "Get off the fucking phone Pascual, and get Alex, now, just do it. I'll wait."

A few moments later Alex's voice came on the line. "Yes? Martin?"

"How about an explanation, Alex?"

He heard Alex cough, clear his throat. "I got a call from Walters in vice on Thursday. He said someone with influence was coming after you, someone he couldn't handle."

"Why didn't you warn me?"

"I might ask you the same question." There was a pause and Martin heard a cigarette being lit in the background, a Zippo clunking. "Martin ... I hear rumours about your dubious choice in girlfriends. And girlfriends' fathers. When you bring the shit down on yourself, you bring it down on everyone. Was it my fault? No. Was it your fault ... ? Right. Now all I want to know is, is it over?"

"It's over."

"Excellent. Then things are back to normal, right?"

"They're normal. But I quit."

"You can't." Alex's voice had certainty in it.

"Why not?"

"Because you've nowhere else to go."

\* \* \*

A few minutes later Maria appeared from the woods, holding the camera. Martin leant over and opened the door for her. She got in and heaved the camera into the back seat. "Careful." Martin muttered, and started the engine.

"Well?" Maria demanded breathlessly. Martin nodded. "God. What if he'd shot you?"

Martin's voice was barely audible. "I don't know."

Maria looked at him more closely. "Are you OK?"

"Yes. Did you film it?"

"I think so."

"Good. Thanks."

"But what's it for?"

"To send him a copy of the part after I gave him the gun."

"Why?"

"Because if I send it to the police and newspapers, he'll have to explain it. And if he doesn't pull the police off my back, that's what will happen."

He picked up the phone and dialled again. "Police? Hello. Listen carefully. I'm calling from the New Concordia Wharf in Rotherhithe — by Tower Bridge. My son has just been playing in the underground garage, he discovered a white package strapped to the bottom of a Mercedes. I believe it belongs to a girl who lives here, Nadeine Charmley. I've just had a look, and I think it might be drugs — but I'm no expert and it might also be explosives. I'm moving my family out right now, and I suggest you move quickly." He replaced the receiver.

## XL

The monkfish crouched before them on the table, segmented, glaring back at the diners with a silent, apocalyptic fury. Luke, following Maria's instructions, had dissected the creature, cooked it, made a sauce, then reassembled the whole in a supposedly attractive culinary presentation. Eliot and Chloe ate desultorily, Suzanne and Luke stared at their plates without touching them.

Since Maria and Martin had left, the house had fallen quiet. There had been no more recriminations. More even than embarrassment, a painful weariness had settled on the remaining members of the party.

When Eliot and Chloe had finished, everybody stared at the remains of the fish, disinclined to say or do anything.

Finally Luke murmured: "Seconds?"

"It's too soon after lunch." Chloe dislodged her glazed stare with a shake of her head and grunted agreement. Luke looked up without much disappointment. "I know." he said. "I feel the same way. I was just interested, really, to see if I could still cook something."

With a scrape of her chair, Suzanne suddenly got to her feet. "Why don't we just go home?" she suggested.

For a moment no one spoke. Then Luke nodded. "All right. But If we wait a while we'll miss the traffic."

I'd rather just go. There's nothing more to do."

Slowly Luke put down his fork. "All right," he said. There was a general rustle of relief.

"Seems to be a consensus," Eliot said slightly apologetically. He had dropped his brazen attitude. Thinking again of money, he was keen to re-ingratiate himself with Luke as soon as possible.

"What are we going to do with this?" Chloe asked hesitantly, looking at the large, untouched fish, absurd in its puddle of mustard sauce.

"Def it." Luke said decisively. With distaste, Chloe found a dustbin bag and emptied the plate into it. The head collapsed amongst dismembered chunks of the body, still gazing back furiously. "Bad luck, fish." Chloe said. But the fish still stared at her. She tied a knot in the bag.

The car was loaded up, the front door locked, and soon the Millhouse was just a blob of stripy white and black in the distance down the lane.

They reached the main road, and Eliot, who had resumed his place at the wheel, turned to his passengers. Luke was beside him in sunglasses. Chloe and Suzanne, in the back seat, were sitting as far apart as possible. "Anyone fancy a quick look at the exhumations?" he asked.

Luke, beside him, looked puzzled. "The Black Dragon bodies, man. Presumably they were found on the premises."

"Jesus!" Chloe exclaimed. "You're sick, Eliot, sick, fucking sick." Eliot guffawed and glanced in the rear view mirror. In the back, Suzanne was motionless. But Eliot thought he saw Chloe's lips twitch in the ghost of a smile. He hoped so.

So they drove away, back to London.

# XLI

Maria began to talk unasked.

She said: "This has been a very strange weekend for me." When Martin did not respond or look up from the wheel, she went on: "I feel like I've changed.

"Why are you telling me?"

"I don't know. I don't ... I'm trying to figure this out in my head, and I feel like ... you could help."

"Why?"

"I helped you," she said. "I'd like your advice in return."

"On what?"

"I'd just like to know what you think."

"I don't think anything."

She looked disappointed.

Martin drove her to the nearest train station. It was a sleepy place, in a sleepy town. But the timetable promised a train to London within the hour. He bought her ticket. "It's better this way," he said.

"You mean, you want to get rid of me, now I've finished helping you?"

"Yes."

"Will you have a coffee with me while I wait?"

"No."

There was a pause. Her voice was cold. "You know, I don't know what'll happen when I get home. It's going to seem so strange now." Martin was silent. "On Friday night, I was sitting there, watching my brother crawling after Eliot, trying to get some stupid job he wanted. He was having a terrible time, but instead of helping him I started to despise him. Because he was afraid. I started to despise my whole family, with their little ambitions and their half-brained certainties. All the hypocrisy and bullshit ... " She shrugged. "And I thought Eliot was somehow better. More exciting, I suppose. That didn't last though. Then you came along."

"And?"

"You're strong. Independent." She looked away for a moment. "What we just did, I don't know. It made me feel good. Like I was really alive. But I look around me and think about going back to school — and it's all like ... death. Living death. I want to fight that, like you do. Not just lie down in front of it like a coward."

Martin was so still and silent she had to prompt him. "Well?"

"I used to say… to people… that everyone should get up and reach for the stars."

"That's exactly what I mean."

"No matter what they found there. Heaven or hell." He looked away. "It was an incredibly stupid idea."

She became sullen. "Well, at least if I accept my feelings I know I'm still alive." She frowned. "Martin, why are you fobbing me off?"

"I'm not. You asked for advice." He summoned up all his strength, took a step towards her, leant down slightly, and looked into her eyes. "My way," he said slowly, "leads nowhere too. Nowhere."

"You're making fun of me."

He shook his head and stared at her. Then he turned and started to walk away. After he had gone four steps she called in a doubtful voice:

"Martin?"

But he didn't turn.

\* \* \*

Martin drove a round-about route towards London, although he was sure no one would follow him. The sky was overcast. He felt a deep and brooding pessimism descend.

Towards six o'clock it grew cooler. He noticed more vehicles on the road. They were frequently old, sometimes bus-like. Then he realized. They were hippies — new age travellers — journeying probably to some rock festival. He passed a group of people walking. They wore colourful but bedraggled clothes and carried cheap bags. They looked like refugees.

He drove on.

The figure on the road was about six and a half feet tall, angular, and thin as a rake. His head was mostly masked under black hair, some of it tied back in a knot. The rest constituted a vast, straggling beard. His dress was an amalgam of ancient Briton and twentieth century surreal, including hand-beaten bangles around each forearm, coloured beads and strangely, a pair of green galoshes. He also wore a bright yellow canvas poncho over a studded leather jerkin. In his arms he carried a pair of dirty, strangely shaped objects which Martin realized, as he came closer, were in fact two wooden legs.

He was standing in the drizzle, a forlorn figure, hitching a lift. It was beginning to rain more heavily.

Martin did not normally give lifts to strangers. He had no intention of stopping now. But at the last moment, as he drew alongside, he braked.

The tall man loped over to the car. He lowered his head and gazed through Martin's window. Then he said in a low drawl: "Are you headed for the stones, man?"

"Stones?"

"The Henge."

"Stonehenge? "

"The dolerites themselves, man."

"I'm going that way."

"Great. All right if I bring my legs?"

"Put them in the boot."

The eyes and hair receded from the window. A few minutes later they were moving again, the stranger peering myopically round the cabin.

"My name is Awrowlth." His tone suggested conspiracy and drama. "Martin." Martin said.

"You take drugs, Martin?"

"Not much."

"I've got these ace 'shrooms here, if you do ... " He reached into a pouch that was one of a number of things attached to his belt.

"Not now, thanks."

"As you wish." Awrowlth tipped his head back and poured a handful of scrawny mushrooms down his throat.

"Where are you from?" Martin asked.

"Orkney."

"Long way."

"Closer the north pole than here, man. By the way, if you see a guy hobbling around in the road with no legs, tell me will you. He's my neighbour."

"The legs in the boot?"

"Right. He got kind of stoned last night. Must've taken off without them. Doesn't matter — we're all going the same way today, right?"

"I guess so."

They drove in silence for some time. Martin noticed that the road was growing busier by the minute. Almost all the vehicles were travelling at low speeds. Martin overtook them at first, then resigned himself to thirty miles an hour. He also noticed that some of them waved when they saw Awrowlth. Awrowlth rarely waved back.

"Listen." Martin said. "I'm going to drop you at the next junction and get on another road. I have to make London tonight."

"Sure." Awrowlth said.

But at the next junction there were police, and the turn off was blocked. Martin indicated his wish to go on, but the police waved him after the others "They're detouring." Awrowlth announced knowledgeably. "Babylon likes to try that."

"What do you mean?"

"They look like they're being real helpful, directing you to the stones, right? In fact they're directing you away from them."

"Well. Do you want to get out then?"

"No need. You'll see."

At the next junction, and the next, there were police forcing the traffic flow in one direction. Then at the next, a coach appeared to have broken down across the road. The police were running around frantically, the traffic was piling up and hooting. The police began to direct cars into the junction. Awrowlth chuckled. "That's called de-derouting. These guys ain't bright. They think we don't have maps."

"Yeah." Martin muttered. "But it's time I got out of here."

"Impossible. Only one way to go now."

"Shit."

"What's wrong, man? You wanted?" Martin looked at him. Awrowlth laughed. "You a ... criminal, or something?"

Martin drove doggedly on. But Awrowlth knew what he was talking about. Between them, the police and the travellers had ensured that the traffic all led one way. And at a certain point the traffic was pulling off the road and parking. Martin said: "I think this is it."

Awrowlth shook his head. "You may as well park. Up ahead nothing's moving, they won't let anyone go forward. And you can't turn back." Martin saw that he was right.

"Dude," Awrowlth said, "go with the flow on this one. Trust me."

Martin parked his car in the field next to a 1959 Bedford dormer and reluctantly joined his companion as he set off, carrying the two wooden legs. The land was soft, undulating, and would soon be mud.

Awrowlth pointed to the top of the incline they were on. "Next hill along," he said.

"Next one?" Martin shook his head. "Jesus."

Again, he noticed that a lot of people seemed to know Awrowlth. They seemed to greet him with some respect. The Dealer, Martin decided. But at the top of the first hill, from where Stonehenge was finally visible, there was a diversion. A huge ring of policemen was forming, apparently trying to stop the many walkers from passing. In the distance a helicopter was circling the stones, lights flashing in the slowly gathering dusk. Beneath it a vanguard of two to three thousand people, some carrying lighted torches, was milling about the site.

"This is where the fun starts." Awrowlth whispered, surveying the angry faces of his fellow travellers and the uncertain but stubborn intransigence of the police. Suddenly a bellow of enormous power broke through the air. No one except Martin looked at Awrowlth. It happened again. It came from Awrowlth, but his lips hadn't moved. They were hidden behind his muff of beard.

Martin looked behind him. To his great distress he saw a column of police in green-yellow dayglo outfits heading up the hill, sandwiching the group of hippies, now some two hundred strong. One of them was yelling something through a megaphone. Then on the left flank, a huge phalanx of men and women, dressed in rags, long haired, appeared. The charging police slowed, surprised. Almost without warning, the fighting began.

Martin shrank back immediately, looking for the centre of the mass. To his amazement, he saw that at least half the travellers were armed. With lumps of stone, catapults, clubs, things which had been concealed under their long clothes. They were pressing forward in a chaotic but purposeful charge. Another helicopter appeared in the distance. The police who had charged up the hill now ran back down it. The megaphone fell silent. Instead, the sound of Awrowlth's explosive, improbably loud voice rang out.

A policeman was hit in the back of the head with a stone. He fell. The crowd surged over him. Martin found himself attached to the movement, unable to go anywhere independently. He almost stepped on the downed policeman, who was on his face in mud. He looked dead.

Then Martin lost his balance, and with a horrible feeling of helplessness began to fall ...

He felt a strong hand grab his collar and yank him up. Awrowlth was standing there. His eyes were shining, but he looked distracted. In his free hand he still carried one of the wooden legs.

"You see ... you see those guys with the full-face helmets? And the big shields?" he said calmly.

"What?"

"Look." Martin looked where he was pointing. At the bottom of the hill were riot police. The dayglo police were running back into their ranks, while the travellers charged pell-mell towards them. Several fires seemed to have burst into life. A large piece of material, possibly a tent, was floating surreally through the air just above them, like a downed Zeppelin.

"You know what they look like?"

Martin managed to shake his head.

"They look like Roman Legionnaires. With the helmets. And the big square shields. Do you see it?"

Martin didn't bother to nod. "And these guys," Awrowlth released him and waved a bony hand, "our people, look at them: they're like the ancient warriors of Wessex. The Anglo Saxons."

Martin winced as he saw a riot policeman slam his baton into the head of a pregnant girl who had run straight into him.

"What the fuck are you doing?" Martin said between his teeth. "You know you can't win!"

"Got no choice. Get beaten up year after year anyhow. Time we fought back. And ... I don't know."

"Don't know what?"

"I don't know. *I* think maybe the time is ripe. These guys are maybe not so tough."

"They've got *guns*."

"Well, that's true ... but ... the Romans had the Testudo, the catapult and the tactics ... didn't do them much good in the end though, did it? Thing is ... *important* thing, if you want my opinion, is, they've lost the will. Right through from the footmen, to the guys who are supposed to direct the footmen. They stopped believing in themselves. *They stopped believing in themselves*. Just like the Romans. You know what it is when people stop being communal and start stepping on each other's toes looking for personal gratification? Decadence. Just like in Rome." He turned and looked at Martin again, once more strangely relaxed and thoughtful. But Martin knew now that it was a veil. "Whereas, as I see it, *we've* got motivation." He grinned, almost mockingly. "Going to build a new world, man!"

Martin finally realized that he had totally misread his companion.

"You see, my friend ... "

Martin found himself blinking under the steady gaze.

" ... it's what I always say faced with the improbable, the impossible, the implausible: Rome fell."

Contact the author: bookman@inbox.com